# Project Moonshadow

**Project Moonshadow**
by Michael Cavendish

First published in 2022

Copyright © 2022 Michael Cavendish

This is a work of fiction. Names, characters, businesses, places, events, locales, and incidents are either the products of the author's imagination or used in a fictitious manner. Any resemblance to actual persons, living or dead, or actual events is purely coincidental.

National Library of Australia Cataloguing-in-Publication data

A catalogue record for this book is available from the National Library of Australia

Cavendish, Michael
Project Moonshadow

ISBN: 978-0-9923655-4-7

# Project Moonshadow
Michael Cavendish

The glare of the flat-panel displays had finally taken its toll. Her eyes ached, her head throbbed, and the images on the screen wavered in and out of focus – it was all rather unsettling. Laura Meadows, 26 and fresh out of college with a PhD in astrophysics, had sat at her desk for nearly nine hours straight and was exhausted. Her dark brown, almost black eyes were tired and dry, and it was becoming hard to maintain focus, let alone concentrate on her work. Her neck and lower back ached, and she desperately needed to pee.

"Why do I get the crap jobs?" she yawned out loud as she leaned back, stretched her arms out and stared up at the panelled fibreboard ceiling above. Thinking she may have been overheard, Laura gingerly peered over the shoulder-high partition of her six by six feet three-walled cubicle to see if anyone had noticed. They hadn't – the place was deserted – not surprising as it was nearly one thirty in the morning, and no currently active missions required twenty-four-hour monitoring. She may have a tedious job – a cryptic request to trawl through thousands of images from several different instruments looking for 'anything' of interest – but she loved her job despite her private murmurs to the contrary.

Laura sat alone in one of the many drab fabric-lined cubicles that made up the analytical section. She yawned again and averted her attention to two little photos she had pinned to her cubicle wall the day she started her job just two months earlier. Both pictures were black and white reproductions of scratched and grainy originals. One was a formal portrait of a balding middle-aged man. With a neatly trimmed moustache, his kind and intelligent eyes stared back at her. The same man also appeared in the other photo, but one would not have recognised him. Dressed in a heavy coat and flat hat, he stood in the snow next to a thin metal frame that wouldn't look too out of place in an old Soviet-era kindergarten playground. The photo, taken on a frigid New England day, was that of Robert Goddard as he stood next to his latest invention – a liquid-fuelled rocket.

Robert Hutchings Goddard was a professor of physics and a pioneer of controlled liquid-fuelled rocketry. He invented and launched the world's first liquid-fuelled rocket on March 26, 1926, and in the years before World War II, he had constructed machines that could attain 550 miles per hour – faster than most people of his time could even comprehend. Often ridiculed for his ideas, Goddard was somewhat a recluse of a scientist. As such, he received far little of the support and recognition he deserved. It was not until after the war that the public began to hear about this brilliant man and his contribution to society. In 1959, some 14 years after his death, Goddard was finally recognised for his genius. That year, Congress authorised the issuance of a gold medal in his honour. However, a more substantial recognition came that same year with NASA's opening of the Goddard Space Flight Centre – a large complex of buildings in Maryland devoted to space research and discovery and the place in which Laura now worked.

As she rubbed her eyes, Laura felt the need for some positive reinforcement. She opened her web browser and selected a page from her list of favourites. Already cached on her computer, the image popped onto the screen the millisecond she clicked the link. The monochrome image that appeared was peppered with craters of all sizes. The craters were bright on the right and dark on the left. This indicated that the Sun was positioned to the left of the scene. With some effort, Laura focused on one of the tiniest craters. It was almost a pinprick on the image, but it had the opposite lighting – it was bright on the left and dark on the right. It wasn't a crater at all but a small mound. The entire image represented an area just over a square kilometre, and it was captured by the Lunar Reconnaissance Orbiter or LRO for short. That little speck of light was the spent landing stage of Apollo 11 in the Sea of Tranquillity. This was the second and more detailed image than the one released to the world in 2009, just prior to the 40th anniversary of landing man on the Moon. She looked more closely at the image and could easily make out the trail that Neil Armstrong made as he skipped about fifty metres towards the Little West crater. She could also identify the location of some of the early science packages left behind.

Laura had looked at that image hundreds of times, and she let out a gasp of wonderment each time – goose bumps rose on the nape of her neck and ran down her spine. Simply amazing, she thought to herself. For a long time, even she had been an Apollo 11 sceptic. Laura knew that Apollos 12 and 14 through 17 must have landed due to the amount of material returned to Earth, but she had always been dubious about that first mission. The race to beat the Russians was considered an imperative. The poor-quality images of those first steps and a commander who was a Freemason and who shied away from the public after the mission all made for a perfect conspiracy theory – several of them, in fact. Seeing the images directly from the satellite feed and after minimal enhancement, she knew for sure that there had been no conspiracy. Neil and Buzz had travelled a quarter of a million miles, landed with less than eight seconds of fuel in the tanks and spent just two and a half hours exploring the surface. This had to satisfy even the harshest of sceptics – or so she had thought. She was mistaken. The conspiracy theorists argued that NASA had airbrushed in detail and would only be satisfied when images taken from another country's satellite showed the landing site. "That would be some time coming," she mumbled, knowing that it would be several years before an Indian or Chinese probe could capture images of similar detail and quality. With the global financial crisis and numerous budget cuts, she was also mindful that the next pair of feet to stand on the Moon were unlikely to be American.

"Hello, my little Lunar Module… looking at that image again!" Laura's heart thumped, and she jerked around to see Brad standing behind her, staring at the screen from over her shoulder and furnishing a broad grin of perfect white teeth.

As her heart rate returned to normal, Laura replied with a stern tone but also with relief in her voice, "I wish you wouldn't creep up on me like that – and don't call me your little landing module; you know how much that annoys me!" On her first day at GSFC, fellow but senior analyst Brad Sommers realised that Laura was fascinated with the Moon and that her initials made for a perfect nickname. Laura cringed at the thought of how annoying Brad would be if he discovered her middle name was Emily. That would make her his little Lunar Excursion Module, no doubt.

"What are you doing here so early… or so late?" Brad replied, seemingly ignorant of Laura's vexation. "You only get paid for a standard week's work. No overtime at the good ol' GSFC."

"I know that, Brad," Laura said as she exhaled. "I just like the work I'm given, even if it is as boring as bat shit. The sooner I'm finished here, the sooner I can get onto something else. Anyway, it's not as if I have a pressing social life."

"I can help you with that." Brad retorted with a grin and a wink. A handsome man, Brad had short blonde hair, a natural glowing tan and a chiselled jaw usually reserved for stars of daytime soap operas. If he didn't have a reputation for being a ladies' man, she might have paid some thought to his jibe.

"Mmm, perhaps when it starts snowing in Hell," Laura responded.

With a widening grin, Brad countered, "So I'm in with a chance then? It's been proven that Hell is cooler than Heaven, you know, and I can take you right to Heaven!"

"Ah, the famous one-track mind we all know and love, Bradley," Laura said, knowing that he hated his full first name and would stifle the conversation.

She was right. Changing the subject, Brad continued, "So, what exactly are you doing with the old LRO imagery?"

"I thought you knew. The boss asked me to review as much lunar imagery as possible and to look for anything interesting," she replied.

"Interesting? What the Hell does that mean?" Brad queried as he grabbed a chair from a neighbouring cubicle and sat down beside her.

"Your guess is as good as mine, Brad. Someone high up wants me to review the whole Moon, one image at a time. It's a strange brief, but the boss gave it to me, and I will do the best I can. I must admit that I initially thought this was some kind of newbie prank – like sending an apprentice out to purchase a long-weight or a sky hook. However,

Simmons tells me that this request comes right from the top. Who am I to argue?"

"Simmons is not the kind of man to haze newcomers. Your dedication is commendable, LM, but do you have any idea who ultimately requested this task?" Brad asked.

"Nobody I know by name, but I remember the boss having a heated discussion with an old grey-haired man wearing an outdated and well-worn suit a couple of days ago. I wasn't quite in earshot, but Simmons mentioned the LRO and about a waste of resources. I'm the only one here still working on LRO data, so they must have been talking about me. The old man must have been quite powerful though, as Simmons had no room to manoeuvre. It may have had something to do with the bodyguard, but I've never seen the boss cave in before."

"Bodyguard?" Brad queried.

"Yes, a very intimidating man, just like the ones you see in the movies. He had a short razor-sharp haircut and wore a black suit, white shirt, black tie, and sunglasses. He looked like an extra from the Blues Brothers movie. Oh, and he wore one of those little earpieces with the curly cord," she responded, twirling her finger around her ear to illustrate the shape of the earpiece cable.

With a little whistle, Brad returned, "Suits and spooks... I wonder if you'll find out what it is all about."

"Well, it would make my job easier…" she replied. Realising the time and caught mid-sentence, she asked, "Brad, what are you doing here so early?"

Searching for words, Brad realised that telling the truth was probably easier than telling a lie. Rubbing his jaw, he said sheepishly, "I just finished a scorching date that ended up a bit cold, if you know what I mean."

Laura could see the faint remains of lipstick on one cheek and the slight redness of a slap mark on the other – she thought it must have been a hard slap. Brad liked to go to his office to lick his wounds and reflect on his remarkable ability to pick up women and piss them off with similar rapidity.

"Anyone I know?" Laura asked with a slight grin.

"Nope, LM... no one from the GSFC... this time," and, after a pause, "I think I'll just go home and get some shuteye. See you in a few hours." With that, Brad left Laura's cubicle and headed for the elevator.

Laura had heard of Brad's famous dates and also about the rumour of his little black book. She was aware of the office gossip that his quest in life was to seduce and bed women with every possible combination of hair, skin and eye colour. I wonder how many ticks he has in his book, she mused. Then another, this time uncomfortable, thought hit her with a shudder. She wondered if he'd ticked the brown-haired, brown-eyed Indian entry yet. Although born in the USA, Laura was only a first-generation American – both of her parents were wealthy immigrants from Kolkata, West Bengal. Shaking off that thought, Laura looked at her watch to discover it was nearly two o'clock in the morning. Realising she could grab a few hours of sleep herself, she switched off her monitor and headed for the elevator with a quick side trip to the bathroom for a much-needed pee.

Leo Helfgott sat in an old but luxurious high-back leather chair and drummed his fingers on the pile of dusty manila folders on his desk. He always tapped his fingers when pondering, thinking, or scheming. At 80 years, Leo showed every bit of his age. He looked weary and tired, with thin grey hair and a face with too much skin for his skull. Leo used to be much larger, but his appetite had waned after the death of his wife. He lost a lot of weight but not that much skin. Every time he looked in the mirror, he had flashbacks of old cartoons of Droopy, the slow-speaking bloodhound. Leo had retired almost five years ago to spend the rest of his days with his wife gardening, sitting about, and generally doing the things that retirees do. However, his Patty had died suddenly only a few months into his retirement, and that left Leo lost – completely adrift. He had reached his lowest ebb and soon discovered that finding ways to occupy the long, lonely days was difficult and required a lot of energy. He had even contemplated suicide, but with the last of his resolve, he realised that what he needed was something to focus on – a mission – an obsession. In the end, it came down to a single book – a tome that he could put his name on that covered the most exciting part of his life – his wartime days at the OSS.

The OSS, or Office of Strategic Services, had a relatively short life. Founded in 1942 and dissolved in 1945, the OSS was the US's first coordinated intelligence agency. Prior to the OSS, American intelligence was run on an ad-hoc basis by the various departments of the Executive Branch, including the State, Treasury, Navy and War Departments. Few people have heard of the OSS, but everyone knows of its direct successor – the Central Intelligence Agency, or CIA.

Leo was there from the beginning – a bright-eyed eighteen-year-old who couldn't go to combat because of flat feet and a slight heart murmur. However, Leo had a great mind and strong mathematical abilities that made him perfect for other duties, including code breaking and strategic information analysis. He excelled at what he did and gradually worked his way up through the ranks of the OSS and then the CIA, ultimately to the position of Deputy Director.

Writing a book about his life was a perfect way for Leo to spend time and reminisce and recount the many untold stories that helped shape the world today. Despite being retired, Leo still had some clout due to his former rank. He had approached his present-day counterpart and told him of his plans. Once Leo had re-assured that the CIA could read and vet the copy before going to press, he was given carte-blanche access to the Agency's archives. It appeared that his security status had not diminished on his retirement. What also surprised Leo was their offer to supply him with an office and some administrative assistance – which he accepted gratefully. Whether it was a coincidence, fate, or irony, the Director of the CIA provided Leo with an office in a red-bricked building at 2430 E Street, NW – A stone's throw from the Kennedy Centre for Performing Arts and the infamous Watergate Hotel. Leo had ended up where he had started – a room in the former OSS headquarters.

Leo had worked on his book for almost four years, meticulously ploughing his way first through the OSS archives and then through those of the early CIA when his assistant delivered a box of files labelled 'Declass. Misc. NFA'. Leo thumbed through these 'declassified miscellaneous – no further action' files whilst sipping pungent black coffee from a souvenir CIA mug. Each manila folder was by a different author and was filled with pages of sketches, hand-drawn maps, abstract scribbles and the occasional handwritten or typed report. Some of the illustrations looked like they came from the hand of a five-year-old, whereas others were more refined.

Leo concluded that these files were obviously unrelated to the OSS or the early CIA days. He looked at the date stamps on the files and noted that they were in no particular order – some were from the late 60s and others from the early 80s. Also, it was clear that these were not official CIA files, as none bore the crest of the Agency. However, whichever project they belonged to was a long-lived one that spanned three decades, and Leo found these files intriguing. It was like a new form of cryptic crossword to him. He read each file in turn and pondered any hidden meaning if indeed there was any.

Of all the people who had files in this archive, the contributions of one, Richard Fairbrother, caught Leo's eye. There was something familiar about his reports – something he couldn't quite put his finger on. A single page intrigued him, but he didn't know why. Something on the page looked familiar, yet out of place. Taking another sip of coffee, it clicked – after a few days of pondering, Leo made the connection that had eluded him. It can't be… it's not possible, he thought. The page contained some rectangles, arrows and other geometric symbols, and the number 2,976 appeared several times, along what looked to be a sketch of a cloud with the word 'Traitor' ominously written above it. He looked at the date on the report – 17 August 1980. Not possible! A chill went up his spine, and the air in the room suddenly seemed much colder. Leo trawled through the archive box and extracted all of the reports by Richard Fairbrother, collated them chronologically and placed them front and centre on his desk.

These documents were much more important than his book, Leo concluded. These files, although long forgotten, were controversial, still topical after so many years and cried out for further investigation.

As he drummed his fingers on the extricated files, Leo cogitated. Were these files lost on purpose? Is Fairbrother still around? What security implications do these files have? What are the political implications? These questions came to mind almost simultaneously, and he mentally cubby-holed them for future reference just as quickly. One question stuck – his book could wait – will they let him follow this through?

# Chapter Three

Neil Simmons sat at his computer and passed his eyes over a long list of numbers as he ran his hand through his white not-quite-military cropped hair. He was a scientist, God damn it. Monthly budgets were for pencil-sharpening Volvo-driving cardigan-wearing accountants and not for people like him. Multi-tasking may be the buzzword that delivers efficiency, but that was all false economy in Simmons' mind. It detracted him from doing his job. Spending half a day on budgets prevented him from doing half a day's meaningful work. What especially riled Simmons was that an accountant could have done the four hours of spreadsheet-based number-crunching in under an hour. Where was the saving there?

Simmons' eyes fixated on one line – Meadows, Laura, salary. Another waste, he thought. A bright kid asked to do something pointless. He pushed his chair away from his computer terminal, swung around and gazed out at the cold and crisp blue sky, and the oranges, reds and browns of the autumn fall caught his attention briefly. His thoughts wandered to his meeting with Helfgott a few days prior. The man may be old, but he was a bulldog regarding getting his way. Perhaps it was just the signed orders from the Vice President of the USA that gave him such authority, Simmons thought. Helfgott gave no indication of which department he represented. The fact that he had a bodyguard and a letter from the Whitehouse led him to assume that it was a concern of the Executive Branch and probably much higher than his pay grade.

"Who is that old bastard?" he breathed out aloud through clenched teeth. He kick-pushed his chair back to the computer, opened up a web browser and began to Google. There were several references to the man concerning intelligence gathering during WWII and the cold war, but very little over the past decade. One search engine result took him to an online store and to a book entitled 'America's Secret War: The Inside Story of the OSS and the Birth of the CIA' by Leo D. Helfgott. Simmons clicked on the thumbnail image of the book to see a larger version of the dust jacket. On the back was a small photograph of Helfgott. The man's a CIA agent, Simmons realised – at least he used to be. Under the image was a short biography of Helfgott that summarised his rise to Deputy Director of the CIA and the fact that he had officially retired in 1999.

Simmons rolled himself back to the window, stared at the sky and started to think. Why would an old long retired CIA agent be interested in high-resolution lunar imagery? Why would the Whitehouse be involved? It didn't make any sense.

Simmons' analytical mind kicked in. Leo was an old but highly-ranked OSS/CIA agent, so his interests must involve post-war technology earlier than 1999 when he retired. The CIA isn't involved in domestic issues, so their focus would be on a foreign power. High-resolution images of the Moon – something must be there which was too small to see prior to the LRO imagery coming online. Pressure from the Whitehouse – it must be important and politically sensitive even today.

Simmons then started to review the technical aspects of other lunar missions that could further constrain the alternatives. Launched in 1959, the Soviet Union's Luna 1 was the first probe not to blow up on launch but missed the Moon by some 6,000 kilometres and entered a solar orbit somewhere between the Earth and Mars. Luna 2, launched in September of the same year, successfully reached the Moon, but it was designed to collide, not land, and would have vaporised on impact. In fact, it was not until 1966 that a probe, Luna 9, achieved a lunar soft landing. Then Simmons began to think about the Lunar Reconnaissance Orbiter. The LRO in its 50km orbit has a resolution of around 50cm, so the target of interest must be at least a metre in diameter if it is to be picked up with any degree of certainty.

Putting it all together, Simmons began to draw a tentative conclusion based on the little information he had. Leo must be looking at an event that put something on the Moon, probably by a foreign power, after 1966. If before 1988, getting anything to the Moon would be possible only by the USA and the USSR. If more recent, then A modified Long March 4 rocket could surely put China into the game but not in the manned sense. Were the Ruskies claiming to have landed a man on the Moon first, or are the Chinese breaking some international treaty on the military use of space? Or is it more recent – do the Chinese have someone up there now? None of these thoughts sat easily with Simmons.

If asked whether China could land their countrymen on the Moon, Simmons would have laughed very loudly. But China's ever-growing strength, not to mention their ingenuity and resourcefulness, saw them put a man, Yang Liwei, into orbit back in 2003. Publicly on the record to set foot on the Moon by 2020, could they have achieved this feat ten years earlier and under complete secrecy? The colour washed from Simmons' face just at that thought. Not long after Yang's adventure, President George W. Bush unveiled an ambitious plan to return Americans to the Moon and to use the mission as a stepping stone for future manned trips to Mars and beyond. It was all bravado and lip service at the start of Bush's second term. Almost a year after the space shuttle Columbia re-entry disaster, this announcement was quite hollow. The entire "Vision for Space Exploration" speech was just a way to soften the blow that the space shuttle fleet was to be retired. Instead of developing new reusable space-plane technology, NASA was to take one giant leap backwards and return to using single-use Apollo-era capsules. Now with the shuttle fleet almost retired, a replacement craft was not ready and wouldn't be for several years, the USA was totally reliant on the Russians for crew and material transfer to and from the International Space Station. He felt sickened and betrayed by the whole matter.

He glanced at his watch and realised it was well after three o'clock – he grabbed the phone and called through to his secretary "Tina, could you get Laura Meadows up here at once, please." With his usual and often misinterpreted abruptness, he hung up the phone without waiting for a reply.

Laura felt like a schoolchild being summoned to the headmaster's office as Tina escorted her to meet with Simmons. Laura knew very little about him except that he was a very intimidating person. What have I done? Am I for the chop? These two thoughts alternated through her mind with each footstep. When she entered his office, Simmons was standing, facing the window and was sipping on a mug of coffee.

Without turning around, Simmons began, "Thank you, Tina, that's all. Laura, please take a seat." He turned around to see that she was still standing – almost to attention. Laura was petite, to say the least, only about five foot two and had a slim but athletic build. She must run a lot, he thought. She had beautifully toned skin and long dark brown hair, and Laura was very attractive even with the little make-up she wore. "Please, sit," Simmons repeated, gesturing to the more comfortable chair on her side of the desk.

Laura was apprehensive and sat down gingerly. "Thank you, sir."

"First off, I'm not the ogre many make me out to be. Second, no need to call me 'sir' Laura. I don't mind 'boss' but hate 'sir'. In the company of others, I am Dr Simmons. When one-on-one, you can call me Neil or Boss." Simmons said with a surprisingly gentle tone.

"Have I done something wrong, sir… Boss?" Laura queried.

"No, quite the opposite – you are probably one of the hardest workers I have met in my many years here. I just want to talk to you about your current project. I noticed you saw some of my conversation with an old gentleman a few days ago. What you may or may not have figured out is that he is the one responsible for your current assignment. I just wish to offer some suggestions to help you complete your task so I can put you onto something much more practical and interesting. By the way, have you found anything of interest yet?"

"Lots of craters," Laura replied. Suddenly, fearing that she had been too flippant, she continued. "The Moon's surface area is only about seven percent of the Earth's, and I am reviewing all of that area at sub-metre resolution. Not knowing what to look for doesn't make things easy."

"What approach have you taken?" Simmons asked, nodding in agreement.

"The latest LRO imagery has all been stitched into a single huge mosaic at the highest resolution. It is possible to view a whole hemisphere at the lowest resolution or a scene representing around 10km square at the highest level of detail. I wrote some code to act as a virtual satellite and to extract images based on my parameters for swath width and inclination. It's like peeling an orange with different-sized knives. My first survey had a large swath width, peeling the skin of that orange into wide strips. That didn't take too long to review. On the next pass, I halved the swath width and so on and for each subsequent pass, I review the data at double the resolution of the previous one."

Simmons smiled as he absorbed the information. Simply brilliant, he thought. "That's an excellent approach, Laura. Given your less-than-detailed brief, you have implemented a very efficient way to wade through the data. However, I have been giving some thought to your assignment and wonder if you wouldn't mind trying something a little different?"

Simmons had piqued Laura's interest, and she was eager for an opportunity to do something other than stare at lunar imagery all day. She edged forward in her chair. "I'm all ears, Boss."

Not wanting to discuss his tenuous conclusions, Simmons kept his discussion purely scientific. "It's clear to me that the old man's interest in the LRO imagery is due to its high spatial resolution. This leads me to believe that the old man wants you to look for something relatively small, probably larger than a metre but less than a kilometre; otherwise, they could have trawled through the Apollo archives. If it is a man-made object, I would say it would be less than 50m in size – around a hundred pixels or so. Perhaps the Russians have established a base up there. Let's hope they aren't looking for a golf ball."

Laura laughed at the golf ball reference. The first American into space and Commander of Apollo 14, Alan Shepard Jr., became the first person to play golf on the Moon. Using a Wilson six-iron head attached to a lunar sample scoop handle, Shepard struck two golf balls, the second of which went out of sight. "What do you suggest, Boss?"

"Well, Laura, we developed a suite of image-processing routines in our attempts to find water on the Moon. As you probably know, these work with sun angles and the like to determine locations of permanent shadows. What you might not know is that the software written for this project is quite extensible. It is matrix-based and relatively easy to insert filters and other pattern-matching algorithms into the code. I suggest you take the opportunity to filter the whole Moon at the highest resolution to look for objects that stand proud of the surface. This process will pull out a load of boulders and many craters' rims and central peaks. However, I think it will also produce images that you can review much more quickly than looking at the raw images. What do you think?"

Laura thought for a few seconds before responding. "I had originally concluded that I was to search for interesting geological... selenological features. I was looking for fractures or faults – especially those with discernible offsets. When we return to the Moon, places such as these would be the most interesting to visit, especially if we plan to have a permanent base there. We would need to find as much of our building and life support materials locally, and selenological diversity would give us our best chance to find the widest range of materials. I must admit that looking for man-made objects never really occurred to me."

"I'm with you on that one, and I may be completely out of the ballpark, but are you interested in this alternative approach?" Simmons queried.

"Most definitely!" Laura responded with genuine enthusiasm in her voice.

"Good. I'll arrange access to the code for you and will get the manuals delivered to your station." Simmons replied as he thumbed through a pile of papers on his desk.

Laura sat for a few more seconds before realising the meeting was over. "Thanks, Boss." She stood up and left the office.

Laura recapped her short meeting with Simmons as she walked back to her cubicle. He's not the bastard people make him out to be. Abrupt, maybe, but definitely not a bastard. Looking for something small on the Moon hadn't occurred to Laura, but Simmons' logic was sound. If they were looking for something more significant in size, the Apollo imagery would have been more than adequate. Man-made – what could be up there? Had the US lost something, or were they looking for something else? Laura realised that she didn't have enough information to formulate any conclusions. A mystery is afoot, she thought, coining Sherlock Holmes. Laura suddenly felt she was at the start of something big and important. Promptly and with purpose, she made her way back to her cubicle.

# Chapter Four

The French-polished mahogany meeting table looked out of place with its immediate surroundings. The group of four men and two women sat at the table within the CIA's secure isolation chamber in a room on the second floor of the CIA's main headquarters in Langley, Virginia. The room had no windows, so laser eavesdropping devices were useless. Apart from the table and chairs, a clear perspex podium, whiteboard and projector, there was little else in the room where one could secrete a conventional bug. The isolation chamber was, in essence, a sizeable triple-glazed Perspex box raised off the floor on rubber-isolated posts to prevent the escape of any recordable vibrations. The room had its own oxygen and battery power supply, and a fine metal mesh within the Perspex acted as a Faraday cage to prevent electronic signals from getting in or out. At least meetings in the chamber were uninterrupted by phone calls.

Bob Dexter, Deputy Director of the CIA and Committee Chairperson, pressed a button on the table and watched as the transparent Perspex walls became frosted. The light was softer now, and the atmosphere more intimate. Bob was the first to speak. "Gentlemen... and ladies, of course, welcome to our second sit-rep. We are still in the very infancy of this project and, as such, there is not much to this situation report. If you turn to the first page of your dossier, you will see a chart and a mark showing where I believe we are currently in the timeline. It has been two months since the commencement of this project proper. During that time, work has progressed steadily at the GSFC, and our mark there appears to be very driven – she routinely pulls double shifts, apparently for the love of the job. However, at this stage, nothing of significance has been identified. Are there any questions?" Dexter scanned around the table with his piercing blue eyes.

"Has there been any more work done that can better constrain the project timeline for us?" asked Janet Cleo, the representative from the National Security Agency.

"Not at this stage." Dexter replied in his usual 'why say ten words when two will do' manner.

Another, more authoritative voice spoke out. "Any idea how long we keep the GSFC out of the loop on this?"

"No, Madam Vice President."

"Any idea when or even if then?" she asked.

Bob Dexter responded, "We do not want to risk tampering with the timeline. There is no doubt that the GSFC will need to become involved at some time in the near future. My thought is that when we reach the next stage of the project, we will need to get Simmons involved. When that is, is anyone's guess – tomorrow, next month, or even next year? When he discovers what all of this is about, he may just become a bit easier to handle. Wouldn't you agree?" Bob gestured to the person to his left for his input.

With a wry smile, Leo Helfgott nodded. Although now in his mid-eighties, Leo looked younger than he did six years earlier. His discovery had rejuvenated him – it had given him a real purpose in life.

"Is there any way we can progress this more quickly?" The voice was that of General Carter, representing the US Air Force.

Dexter replied. "General, we have given due consideration to that, and if we don't get anywhere in the next four weeks, we may have to intervene. At this stage, we really do not want to interfere with the process for reasons outlined in the original brief. What I do know is that when we reach the next phase, we are going to require a significant injection of funds. If we want to keep this project a secret, we will have to work out a damn good cover story. Any more questions?" He scanned the room. "Unless there is a breakthrough, our next meeting will be in four weeks. My PA will be in touch to coordinate schedules. Thank you all for your time. Meeting adjourned." With that, he pressed another button on the table. The room's walls became transparent, and a green light on the ceiling changed to red.

# Chapter Five

With his book research on hold, Leo sat at his desk with one of Richard Fairbrother's folders opened and its contents spread out. With an almost blunt pencil, he made notes on a yellow legal pad and summarised the pertinent points of each page. He mused at what the project financiers must have thought of the contents of these reports, if you could call them that. There was a knock on the door.

"Come in," replied Leo.

Leo's assistant, a young, well-dressed lady with androgynous short blonde hair and wearing a pantsuit, entered the room. "I've tracked down an address for you, sir," she said and placed a post-it note on his desk, "it's not far from here in Herndon."

"Well done, Susan. Would you be able to take me there today?"

"I think so. I'll have to arrange a car from the pool, but that should not be a problem."

Leo nodded, and Susan left. Leaning back in his chair, Leo closed his eyes and wondered what lay ahead. Would he find answers, more questions, or something he feared the most – a brick wall?

Later that same afternoon, Leo sat in the back seat of the black Ford Taurus. The day was warm, and the seats' leather was uncomfortably so. He felt uneasy as his anticipation rose. Susan was driving. They turned left from Dranesville Road onto Ridgegate Drive and right onto Thurber Street and pulled-up outside a moderately sized two-storey house with dormer windows and a neatly trimmed front lawn. Susan stepped out of the car and opened the door for Leo. Old age is a bastard, he thought as he shuffled himself around and managed to get his feet out of the car. Fortunately, Susan lent an arm for him to grab hold on. After a bit of wriggling and finally out of the vehicle, they made their way to the front door. A little brass plaque under the doorbell read "Fairbrother Residence". Leo pressed the button.

After a few seconds, a woman in her late thirties opened the door. In her arms was a small child who stared around vacantly as he chewed on a cookie.

"Can I help you?" the woman asked.

Leo responded, "Would it be possible to speak with Richard Fairbrother, please?"

"I'm sorry, but I'm afraid my father passed away several years ago. May I ask you who you are? Did you know him?"

The disappointment on Leo's face was evident. "No, I have never met your father, but I wish I had. My name is Leo Helfgott, and I – I am doing some research for a book." Leo could see the woman was confused. No, she was not confused; she was searching her memory.

"Helfgott?" she asked.

"Yes, Helfgott, it means the health of…,"

"The health of God." the woman interrupted.

"Exactly," Leo confirmed.

"This may sound strange," the woman said, "but I think my father may have left something for you before he died." She took a step back, invited them both into her house, and escorted them to the lounge. "Please take a seat – I'll be back in a moment."

Leo and Susan sat down on a rather luxurious white leather sofa. After a couple of minutes, the woman returned without the child, holding a thick yellow envelope instead. Leo spoke, "Thank you for letting us into your home, but would you be kind enough to tell us your name."

"Sorry, where are my manners." the woman responded. "My name is Lisa Fairbrother. Richard was my father."

"I am sorry for your loss. Did you say that Richard left something for me?"

"I think so. It's the strangest thing. My father died back in 1997 of Alzheimer's. In his last few years, he became quite a recluse and spent a lot of his time in his study. About a year before he died, there were times he was quite lucid, and on one of those occasions, he gave me this." She held out the envelope. "He was adamant that I keep this package for the lion and the health of God. I asked him what he meant, but he would not elaborate. He simply said that I would know when the time had come. Leo – lion, Helfgott – Health of God. I guess the time has come." She handed over the envelope. On the envelope was written in fountain pen; *to the lion with the health of God, make the most of it, RF!*

Leo accepted the envelope that Lisa had offered. "Thank you. Do you have any idea what's in here?"

"None at all. My father was quite strange towards the end. He spent countless hours in his den scribbling and writing notes. Most of it ended up in the trash, but everything he kept he put in that envelope. We all thought it was part of his dementia. I never thought the day would come when I would actually pass this material on to someone. Any idea what's it all about?"

"Not at this stage. I am in the dark as much as you are," Leo replied.

Leo and Susan stood up, and Leo thanked Lisa for her help.

Leading them to the door, Lisa asked, "You will let me know if you get something useful out of that envelope? It would be good to know that my father wasn't as ill as we thought he was towards the end."

"Of course I will." Leo lied. He knew that if any of this material were relevant, it would be instantly code-word classified above top secret.

In the back of the car, Leo's hands trembled as he opened the envelope. He quickly flicked through the 150 pages or so of sketches and handwritten notes. Each page was numbered and dated in the top-right corner. Many of the pages looked pure gobbledygook, but he could see structure in some of the material even if he didn't understand the content. It was like a giant puzzle crying out to be solved. He knew he was just the man to do it.

Leo had a nasty habit that he had had since he was a child. Whenever he read a book, he always found himself on the last page within a few minutes of starting. Today was no different, and he and he pulled out the final page of Fairbrother's notes. The contents of that page shook him to the core – it wasn't gibberish – it was a stark message. He felt sick and uncomfortable. He closed his eyes and thought about Richard Fairbrother – who he was and how he had developed his skill. It's too fantastic to be real, he thought. The gentle rocking of the car made Leo tired – he knew he was old and that afternoon naps were a part of the process. However, the prospect of what lay in those papers had given Leo an adrenalin kick. He began to scan each page from the start, placing each back into the envelope when finished. What Leo saw on page twelve shocked him for the second time in as many minutes. His hands trembled as he looked over the following few pages. He put the notes back in the envelope and asked Susan if she could get him back to the office as quickly as possible.

# Chapter Six

Laura had spent much of the weekend reading the software manual that Simmons had delivered to her cubicle. After reading the manual from cover to cover, she experimented with extending the program's functionality. She successfully created some plug-ins that added new filtering functions to the software, but she was having trouble with the following and most crucial step – automated feature extraction.

The whole area of artificial intelligence, AI, had advanced in great leaps and bounds in recent years but was still in a very early stage of development. For humans, identifying a square object in a pile of round ones is a simple task, but for a computer, it's not so easy. You must teach a computer how to see from a series of still pictures. The computer then needs to learn to differentiate between objects and classify them. Finally, a context needs to be created to allow the computer can do its work. If the things on the image are cleanly separated, then an AI program can be very accurate. However, if any of the objects overlap, the system would falter, and a whole heap of new code would have to be written to cover the added complexity of the system.

Totally stuck, Laura conceded defeat and flicked to the support page of the manual to see who could provide help, and she received a shock when she saw the name. The chief programmer of the software was none other than Dr Bradley Sommers. She knew that underneath his ego and antics that he was a nice person, but she found it hard work to deal with him. Now or never, she thought. She peered over her cubicle wall and saw the top of Brad's head in his cubicle. Laura opened the instant messenger application on her computer and fired a short line of text to Brad's computer – 'Houston, LM has a problem – needs assistance from CapCom'.

Within a few seconds, she had a reply. 'OK to video-chat?' A couple of seconds later, Brad's image appeared on her screen, along with a request to start a chat session. She clicked the icon to accept the connection.

"Hi, Brad." Laura started. "You look a little tired – too much trick or treating last night?"

"You could say that." Brad's response was subdued – probably the result of another disastrous date.

"Brad, I'm using your feature extraction software on the LRO imagery and trying to add an automated extraction routine, but I keep crashing the program. I can create conventional and adaptive convolution filters with no issues, but I haven't been able to go much further. Would you be able to help me?"

"No problems, Laura. I'll be with you in a few minutes."

"OK, thanks," Laura replied. Before she could say anything else, Brad had closed the chat session. Definitely another date gone wrong, she concluded.

Several minutes passed before Brad turned up at Laura's cubicle. When he arrived, Laura noticed that he was immaculately dressed, as always, but he looked down – forlorn even. "Are you OK?" she asked.

"I can't say I am, Laura. Whenever I think something good is on the horizon, I discover that it's just someone heading my way to kick me in the balls."

"Bad date?"

"Two bad dates, actually. The problem was that both dates were at the same restaurant."

"What! Did you try to have consecutive dates at the same restaurant? Don't tell me they met each other at... changeover time?"

"Worse," Brad replied with some embarrassment.

"How could it possibly be worse?"

"Well, I sort of made a bit of a mistake. I had met Helen at the squash courts... beautiful thing and another Helen online... she's a feisty little minx. I got my wires crossed, and to cut things short, they both arrived at the restaurant at the same time and asked the Maitre d' for my table simultaneously."

"Sounds bad – I guess you felt a bit outnumbered." Laura couldn't help but smile.

"It gets worse." Brad was starting to lighten up and see the comic nature of the situation. "I was already at the table when they both came over. I was shocked but strangely aroused as well, come to think of it. I ended up with a glass of ice water in my lap and one over my head."

Laura slapped Brad's arm on the 'aroused' comment. "Brad, I think you just witnessed karma in action."

"I think you may be right there, LM. What's your problem with my code?"

Laura was always amazed by Brad's behaviour. Not so much by his string of bad dates and short-lived romances, but by his ability to switch from court jester to serious analyst at a flick of a switch. Laura explained to Brad that she was interested in locating objects that protruded from the Moon's surface – boulders, lunar modules and the like. She also demonstrated that she understood how to import new filters into the software but was having problems writing code for the feature extraction component. "I just don't know how to write feature extraction code at such a low level and splice it into your software." Laura summarised.

While Larua was talking, Brad stared intently at the computer screen and twirled a pencil around the fingers of his left hand. "Laura, you'll want to use our high-res digital elevation model of the Moon. It was created from LRO's stereo narrow field cameras, so there are no geometric distortions that can throw things off. However, based on what you want to do, I don't think you even need to write any new code. Your filters do a good job of removing the low spatial frequencies in the imagery. I think that ANN code can do the feature extraction for you after you create a few more derived layers for input – sun azimuth and some common morphological ones come to mind."

"Anne?" Laura asked, looking puzzled.

"No, A. N. N. – artificial neural network. I compiled a whole heap of open-source code into the program. I never really needed to use it during the LRO and LCROSS missions, but it's all tested and ready to go. I would suggest using a basic back-propagation approach first, and if that holds no joy, move on to more complicated methods." Brad responded.

Laura had heard of artificial neural networks – systems that attempted to learn by example. Over the past few years, neural networks had become widely used and even embedded in many common appliances, from parking machines to fingerprint readers. Brad spent a few hours introducing Laura to the technology and how to create artificial neurons, training sets for the ANN to learn from, and test sets to see how well they did. Laura was amazed at Brad's depth of knowledge, drive, and enthusiasm. She was also astounded that he could easily switch off his ego – he seemed a totally different person. He really is an enigma, she thought.

Laura had learned much from Brad and now had enough to go on to complete the task solo. Realising he had done enough explaining, Brad stood up. "If you have any problems, LM, just holler. Oh, I do need to stress that you don't over-train the network." Brad continued. "You will think that you have created a good net, but you will discover that it only applies to the training data and is pretty much useless when applied to the other data. If you create good test sets, you will easily identify if the net is overtrained."

"Thanks for all of your help, Brad. I really appreciate it." Laura said as Brad left the cubicle.

Brad responded with a backward wave of his hand.

It was almost end-of-business when Laura had completed filtering a small portion of the lunar imagery. From the original LRO imagery, Laura had created several layers showing different aspects of the underlying data. As a training set, she picked the locations of four of the six Apollo landing sites – the other two went into one of the test sets. She also identified numerous boulders and other features on the Moon's surface. Some of these went into the training set and the others into the test sets.

After a couple of hours of tweaking various parameters and doing small test runs, Laura felt she was ready to train the network proper. As a starting point, she decided to use the network structure Brad had created earlier in the day. With a sense of apprehension, Laura clicked on the 'TRAIN ANN' button and watched the display show the progression of how well the network was learning. The 'percent trained' entry started very low but, within a few iterations, jumped to 80% and then to 90%. After a couple of minutes and over a hundred iterations later, training hovered around the 95% mark. Now and then, the value would drop to the mid-80s and begin to climb again. This was a standard trick to help prevent over-training the data: the software injected random noise into the inputs to juggle things and avoid so-called local maxima traps.

At 95.4% trained, Laura clicked the 'STOP TRAINING' button. That's good enough for a first pass, she guessed. The screen then displayed the learning parameters derived from the training data. She then fed in the first test set, and the result was returned to her within seconds. A glance at the output showed that the training had been somewhat successful. The neural net had bulls-eyed both Apollo landing sites in the test set and a significant number of boulders, including the central peaks of most craters that had them. As the training was not perfect and was unlikely to be, there were many false negatives and positives in the result. A false negative was where the net failed to identify a feature where one exists, and a false positive was the opposite. Optimistic that she was on the right track, she fed in the data for one complete swath of LRO imagery. Having selected a file, she clicked the button to start the network. The progress bar that appeared was less than encouraging. It moved so slowly that it would take an hour or two to complete. She looked at her watch – it was just before 10:30 PM. In two minds about whether to stay, Laura stood up to see if anybody was still around. As usual, the place was deserted. An early night it is, then. Laura switched off her displays and headed for the car park.

The car park was only a short walk from her building and was empty save for a few pool cars. Laura fumbled through her handbag for her car keys. Grabbing the familiar shape of the remote fob, she pressed the button that unlocked the door. Throwing her bag onto the passenger seat, Laura got into the driver's seat and gazed at her reflection in the mirror of her sun visor. She looked tired. She knew that she was a bit of a workaholic but was only now beginning to realise that it had started to take a toll on her looks. She had panda eyes. Next week I must start to work more regular hours, she thought. She flipped her sun visor up, started the engine, checked her rear-view mirror, reversed out of her bay and began the short drive home. Even though the car park and roads around the GSFC were well-lit, she didn't notice the nondescript white van, with headlights off, which followed her out of the car park.

# Chapter Seven

Leo Had spent two whole weeks trawling through the papers that Lisa Fairbrother had given him, looking for anything of significance or relevance. Leo perused the document as a whole and then collated the pages based on potential topical similarities. Leo had identified over a dozen such groupings, and he carefully built up a list of observations for each of these. Some of Fairbrother's notes were so cryptic that he doubted even he would ever understand them. Lisa had explained how prolific her father was – even when suffering visible signs of Alzheimer's disease. Even though Fairbrother had placed items into the envelope during times of clarity, Leo conceded that some pages might be the result of dementia-related confusion and/or delusion.

Leo flicked through the dozen pages of notes and observations he had written. He concluded that Richard Fairbrother possessed a peculiar and powerful gift – Alzheimer's or not. Better now than never, he thought. Leo phoned his assistant and asked for a meeting with the CIA's Deputy Director at his earliest convenience.

Bob Dexter poured a nip of bourbon from a hipflask into his coffee as he stared at the plasma display on his wall that relayed all the latest intelligence flash messages from around the world. It's a slow day, he concluded as he took a sip of his laced coffee. Bob drank very little alcohol but enhancing his afternoon coffee was a vice he had picked up one cold night from a covert listening post in the Tien Shan Mountains of the Kyrgyz Republic. Stationed with an agent from Williamsburg, he was introduced to and fell in love with the Kentucky version of an Irish coffee. Initially drinking it only on cold nights, Bob had taken to having just one every afternoon as a pick-me-up.

The intercom on the desk beeped, and Dexter tapped the receive button. "Yep?" he responded.

"Leo Helfgott is here to see you, Mr Dexter," came the reply.

"Send him in, please," Dexter responded and flicked the intercom off. He then pressed another button that turned the plasma display off.

The door opened, and Leo made his way to Dexter's desk. With no invitation but the privilege of age, he sat down and breathed a sigh of relief. In his hand, he held a thin manila folder.

"Leo, how are you? I expected to see you with a large manuscript for me to read." Bob said with sincerity as he eyed the folder that Leo held.

"Well, Mr Dexter," Leo began, "my research has taken a bit of a turn, and I've stumbled onto something quite intriguing."

"Leo, you know better. Please call me Bob. Now, what's intriguing you?" Bob sat forward with his head resting on his hands while Leo explained the accidental delivery of the box of declassified material and the papers it contained.

Leo concluded, "I have no understanding of the origin of these files and cannot see how they can contain what they do, but I believe they deserve scrutiny."

Bob leaned back in his chair and replied, "This sounds like something out of the X-files. I assume that you're holding one of the files?" He pointed at the folder in Leo's hand.

Leo nodded and handed it over. "This was the file that originally grabbed my attention – the first page, in fact."

Bob looked at the file's cover. The stationary was right for the time – heavy coarse fibre paper, which at the top-right was stamped Project Grill Flame – Army INSCOM. The words 'TOP SECRET' were embellished in large red text on the cover. This had been crossed out and stamped with the words 'DECLASSIFIED' along with a date and signature. Listed on the cover were the names of people who had accessed it, along with dates and their initials. He had never heard of any of them.

"Mmm, Army INSCOM – what would files from the Army Intelligence and Security Command be doing in our archives?" Dexter muttered out loud as he opened the file. "You made sense of this?" he asked as he flicked through the pages of scribbles and hand-written notes.

"It isn't difficult when you have a context to work with, and I can guarantee that this context did not exist when this file was created and even when it was last viewed. Look at the first page and think of the year 2001 – I'm sure it will come to you."

Bob Dexter turned back to the first page and stared at the page. It took a while, but Leo was right; it did come to him. He noticed the date at the top of the page and looked at the file's cover to confirm. With a look of disbelief, he asked Leo, "Does this mean what I think it means?"

Leo nodded. "Yes, I believe that it depicts the 9/11 terrorist attacks on the twin towers in New York City as well as the attack on the Pentagon."

Bob stated back at the paper in amazement – it all made sense. Two slender rectangles, one with a tick coming out of one of the ends, definitely represented the World Trade Towers, even down to the antenna on top of the north building. Holding the paper upright, these rectangles were horizontal as if they had fallen. Not physically accurate but was nevertheless an adequate representation. In one corner was a series of geometric shapes – circle, triangle, square, pentagon, hexagon, and so on. However, the pentagon shape had been drawn over so many times that the pen had almost worn through the paper. "What's the significance of 2,976?" Bob asked.

"I did a bit of super-sleuthing on the Internet – what a remarkable tool that is! It only took me a minute or two to discover the significance of 2,976. It is the official death toll for the 9/11 terrorist attacks."

"Leo, if you had told me rather than showing me, I would have thought you had lost your marbles. How much more material do you have?"

"Well, I thought I was going insane too, Bob," Leo replied with a guttural chuckle. "There is the one archive box that was delivered to me by mistake. I don't know if there are any more where that one came from. There were files from several different people, but only the ones, about a dozen or so, from a Richard Fairbrother stood out."

"Anything in particular?"

"Only the 9/11 one jumped out at me, but there is definite structure to all of his work. I believe it all deserves further analysis. However, what interested me the most is what is not in the Agency's files." Leo explained that although Richard Fairbrother had passed away long ago, he had tracked down his daughter, who for many years had been holding a package for Leo.

Bob gave out a 'bomb-drop' whistle. "That's spooky, Leo. Are you sure you never met this guy years ago?"

Leo replied with a shrug of the shoulders and a shake of his head, "I don't believe so. My official diaries from my CIA days will be archived somewhere – perhaps they can be reviewed – I need to get my hands on them anyway for my book." Leo continued, "The parcel contained over 150 pages of sketches, notes and the like, and I have spent the past couple of weeks going over them. Many topics are apparent in the notes, but one is particularly interesting. Frankly, it scares the bejesus out of me." Leo handed over copies of a couple of Fairbrother's pages and a half-page summary of his observations.

Dexter placed the two pages on his desk side-by-side and kept hold of Leo's note. His eyes bounced between the two. Occasionally his brow furrowed. After a few minutes, his eyes widened, and his mouth fell agape. "Leo, this is all legit, isn't it? You're not pulling a prank on me?"

"You have my word on that, Bob," Leo responded solemnly.

Dexter flicked his intercom button, "Peta, could you please hold all calls and clear the rest of my schedule for today." He looked at Leo, "I hope your book can wait; we've got some work to do."

Leo nodded with satisfaction but played his best poker face to Dexter.

# Chapter Eight

Laura was almost out of breath when she got to her cubicle. She threw her bag under the desk with such force that it hit the partition with a noticeable thud. She dropped into her chair and switched on both monitors. The processing she had left running from the previous night had taken just under two hours to complete. This is going to take forever, she thought. She opened the resultant image. What she saw surprised her; it was completely black. She felt dejected until she began to zoom in and saw specs of grey and white. She knew from what she had read in the manual that black areas were where the ANN did not find a match, and the white areas represented a good match. Areas of grey were simply areas where the ANN could not make up its mind. These areas represented partial matches. She also knew from her image processing classes at university that the eye was more attuned to picking up dark objects against a bright background at short distances. She inverted the image to display its negative and zoomed in to 25% magnification. Laura could see the entire area peppered with boulders and other raised objects. She changed the display's colour so that the output of the ANN was shown in red and overlaid the actual LRO image with 50% transparency so she could see both datasets simultaneously. Although weary at the volume of work required, she expressed some relief that the ANN seemed to be working and had identified boulders, central peaks of craters, and even a lunar lander. Laura jumped when a window popped up on her screen that requested a video chat with Brad. She clicked the 'OK' button, and Brad's face appeared.

"Good morning, LM. How did the processing go last night?" Brad asked with a cheery smile.

The disappointment in Laura's voice and eyes was apparent. "Hi Brad, the ANN did a reasonable job, but it took nearly two hours to process a tiny scene, and it has identified thousands of targets – I'm still going to have to review the entire Moon at the highest resolution."

"Don't worry about processing time – I know how we can speed things up there. However, the number of identified targets is a problem. We will need to refine the network. We can better filter the results if you know what you are looking for. Remember, this first attempt was to find things that stick out of the surface. We can refine that by including factors such as height, aspect ratio or morphology. You can even use the outputs of several neural networks as inputs to others. All it takes is patience and persistence. I've got a whole heap of nets I used on the Mars data some time ago. I can flick these onto you if you like. They are all documented and can easily be adapted to the LRO imagery."

"Yes please, Brad." Laura replied. "I feel overwhelmed by this task, especially with its broad focus and lack of clear objectives," Laura replied and continued to fill Brad in on her discussion with Simmons.

"It sounds to me like they are grabbing at straws. However, based on what was said, I suggest you need to look at a few things. First, you need to look for symmetry in features; second, the aspect ratio of features; and third, the geometry of features. Anything man-made is likely to be round or have nice straight edges. We run the nets and use slice filters to highlight the most anomalous targets first. The good news is that all the routines are in the stuff I'll send you. You will have to tweak these to regenerate nets for the LRO imagery. I can help you with that if you like."

Laura felt slightly reassured by Brad's enthusiasm. "Thanks, Brad. I need all the help I can get. But we are still stuck with the actual time to process the data – it will take thousands of hours."

"Have faith, LM. On your computer, it'll take thousands of hours, but far less if we BOINC it!" Brad answered.

"What? Are you being rude?" Laura replied, looking quite puzzled.

Brad replied with a 'tut-tut' sound and replied. "BOINC – Berkeley Open Infrastructure for Network Computing. It's an open-source volunteer-run system for grid or distributed computing. People on the Internet all over the world volunteer their idle computer time to process large datasets. Each computer is fed a bite-sized piece; when completed, they send the result back and ask for another piece. It's a simple concept but a very powerful one. Probably the most famous setup is the one used by SETI. You know – the group of trekker nerds that look out for signals from little green men. When I last checked, they had over three million computers helping them to filter and process the data they receive from the Arecibo dish in Puerto Rico. Although we have far fewer volunteer computers – they number in the tens of thousands – they are sitting there just waiting to process our data. I would estimate that you could see a two- or three-thousand-fold increase in image turnover. You could probably process the whole Moon in a couple of days."

Although Laura had never heard of BOINC and would never admit it, she was a member of SETI@HOME and routinely left her personal computer on while she was at work or overnight to process their data. She felt uplifted, realising that the task may not be as daunting as she had feared. "That's great, Brad." The relief in her voice was unmistakable.

"I've just dropped the code into your public drop folder. I don't have anything important on today. If you like, I can pop by in half an hour or so and give you a hand."

"I'd appreciate that, Brad," Laura said as she ended the video chat session.

As promised, Brad went to Laura's cubicle and immediately got down to work. Laura quickly began to realise how hit-and-miss creating ANNs can be. Because of the randomness introduced into the system, no two iterations of the same training data ever produced identical results. It was just like asking five experts their opinion on a topic – they always came up with six or more different answers. A few hours passed by as if it were only a few minutes. Brad typed furiously on the keyboard and struck the enter key with a bit of a flourish. "I think that's it, LM. This model takes into effect sun azimuth and declination, estimated feature height from our DEM, and morphological and geometric aspects as well. I've adapted my old code to search for features with regular geometry and those with large aspect ratios – either horizontally or vertically. Finally, I've also included an automated line extraction routine. It uses Sobel filtering so that it can work on quite poorly defined edges. Now for the test!" Brad said as he continued working on Laura's computer.

Although she had been quite involved in the process and offered some excellent ideas, she felt like a sorcerer's apprentice. But she was also relieved that help was at hand. Without Brad, she would have been out of her depth. It would have taken weeks, if not months, of research and trial-and-error programming to get her to where she was.

"And there we have it," Brad said triumphantly. I executed the routines on a small dataset, and it worked flawlessly. "Now let's take one grid of lunar data and BOINC it. Then, LM, I think you can buy us some lunch."

"Lunch. I think I owe you dinner." Laura replied.

"Really?" Brad responded with a raised eyebrow.

"Please take your head out of the gutter, Brad. I mean as colleagues and as a thank-you." Laura replied with a smile.

Brad tapped a few more buttons and hit the enter key. "Let's go, Laura. I hear today's meatball day in the canteen."

Water off a duck's back, Laura thought with a shake of her head. And with that, they both headed for the elevator.

An inconspicuous white van was parked down a side street less than 500m from Laura's cubicle. In relative darkness in the back of the vehicle, a lone figure sat on an old fruit box with one earpiece of a headphone set cupped to his ear, listening. Laura's voice could be heard, but it trailed off. A few seconds later, all he could hear was incoherent office chatter. He stopped recording, and under the dim red glow of his listening post, he grabbed his tattered spiral notebook and reviewed the observations he had made over the past few days. With a nearly blunt 2B pencil, he scribbled his latest findings onto a crumpled and dog-eared page.

# Chapter Nine

Ran Kai Rong held a prestigious post as Administrator of the China National Space Administration. At 38, he was very young for the role he had been given, due in no small part to the coveted positions his parents held in the Communist Party hierarchy. In public, Ran toed the political line of the government. Privately, however, he was a pure capitalist and craved all of its trappings. Outside of his home, the only hint of his love for most things western was the Hugo Boss suits and Salvatore Ferragamo shoes he wore to work each day. If he must be a communist, he could at least be a smart one.

China was in a historical phase of its evolution, and Ran could feel something extraordinary was on the horizon: It was his destiny to be a significant part of it. China's economic might was being felt worldwide and it was close to global recognition as the next great superpower. Ran was a realist and considered the significance of space exploration as much a status symbol as a philanthropic pursuit. After World War II, the Soviet Union became a dominant power when they, too, harnessed the atom. However, their influence started to decline when they lost the space race. Within 20 years of Armstrong walking on the lunar surface, the Berlin wall had crumbled, and a couple of years later, the Soviet Union had dwindled to extinction. Ran knew that if the next pair of feet to stand on the Moon were Chinese, then his great country would have secured its place as the world's second superpower of the 21st century. With the people's will, they would even surpass the Americans… in time.

China was relatively new to space exploration. Their first look towards the Moon began only a few years earlier, in 2007, when Ran witnessed China's first lunar probe launch. Named after a legendary Chinese Goddess, Chang'e-1 surpassed mission expectations by six months and relayed much valuable information to Earth.

Chang'e-1 contained no fewer than twenty-four pieces of equipment, including CCD stereo cameras, high-energy and solar particle detectors, a laser altimeter and imaging spectrometers. The purpose of this launch was three-fold. The only factor that interested the public was proving that China could get a probe to the Moon. The other two goals were scientific. The Moon needed surveying for areas of interest and potential landing sites. Also, if men were to be sent there, any hazards, especially those involving high-energy particles, needed to be identified and quantified. The crews of Apollo missions were the first to report unusual visual phenomena associated with space flight. Outside Earth's protective magnetic field, high-energy high-mass particles induced flashes and visual sensations through their interaction with the retina or the brain's visual cortex. Six successful landings proved that man could survive the trip; many of those astronauts were still alive and showed no ill health. However, China was planning a more extended stay on the lunar surface than the 75 hours managed by the crew of Apollo 17. In all likelihood, any prolonged stay on the Moon would require the creation of an artificial magnetosphere to deflect potentially damaging ionising radiation. In the nearly fifty years since Gagarin became the first person in space, so much has been learnt. However, Ran Kai Rong knew there was much more still to be discovered and understood.

Ran was transfixed on the report he was reading. It was a list of potential landing sites for the next phase of China's lunar exploration programme – robotic rover reconnaissance. The information contained several possible places of interest, but out of them, one, in particular, grabbed his attention. This location was an enigma. It showed some interesting structures that defied explanation. Ran knew that an inconspicuous landscape photographed with the Sun at a particular angle can cause the eye to see things that simply were not there – just like the infamous 'face of Mars' captured in 1976 by NASA's Viking 1 spacecraft. Dozens of books and videos were written on this feature. Even images from the more advanced Mars Global Surveyor craft that proved beyond any doubt that the feature was just a naturally formed mesa did not prevent more books and DVDs on the 'face' from being published.

Is this a natural feature, Ran pondered. His report showed three images of the area, each with the Sun in a different position. Each image appeared to strengthen the argument that the feature was real and not caused by unusual lighting conditions. Have the Americans been doing things on the Moon in secret? Have they been keeping everyone in the dark? If so, then this is the obvious target, Ran thought. There is something of significance here. We have the opportunity to prove ourselves to the world and embarrass the Americans at the same time. What a good day that will be! Ran smiled at that thought.

Ran closed his eyes tightly and imagined the day a fellow countryman stepped onto the lunar regolith. The lunar rover was almost ready, and construction of the first Apolloesque three-stage rocket was well underway. However, at least two launches were needed to test all aspects of the system before astronauts could land on the surface. The first test launch was under a year away, and the ultimate mission was an excruciating five years into the future. Five years ahead of schedule but still five years away. If only he could launch today.

# Chapter Ten

Bob Dexter had been introduced to Fairbrother's work only a few hours earlier. However, he had learnt a lot about him and his work. Bob had arranged an in-office lunch for Leo and himself and asked his assistant, Peta, to pull some files from the archives. He was currently reading these while lunching on a salami and lettuce sandwich.

After finishing the report and sandwich, Bob moved the plates of crumbs and crumpled napkins to one side and handed a new printout to Leo. "Leo, first things first – you are a long-retired agent..."

Leo immediately thought the worst – he was about to be kicked out of the investigation. "but..."

"Please let me finish... and take that look of despair off your face. You are long retired, but I wish to reinstate you under our reserve-activation clause. You will be considered a contractor to the CIA, but you will be afforded the same level of clearance you enjoyed when you had my position. As a contractor, we will recompense you for your time."

"Thank you, Bob," Leo replied with noticeable relief in his voice. "The money is unimportant to me, but this Fairbrother situation consumes me. I know significant findings will come from this – it's in my gut."

"I don't know how or why, but I think you might be right. Please sign the form, and then I can start talking to you about what I have discovered." Bob responded.

Without reading the contract, Leo signed and passed it back.

"Not reading something the CIA hands you to sign – you must really be eager, Leo!" Bob quipped and placed the contract in his top drawer. "OK, now that we are all above board, I can start. Project Grill Flame was one of six that operated contiguously from 1977 to 1995.

Originally conceived by Army Intelligence and Security Command and then by the Defense Intelligence Agency, we finally ended up with the task of reviewing the findings of these projects. We know these under the umbrella of Project Star Gate."

"Like the television show?" Leo asked with a smile.

"No, not like the show, Leo. Project Star Gate goes back further than 1977 – to the late 60s. Intelligence sources showed that the Soviets employed psychics as a potential espionage tool. They spent serious roubles on how to use the paranormal to their advantage. Back then, we would try anything to get one over on the Ruskies, so we initiated a few projects of our own. Even Uri Geller, the spoon-bending guy, was involved."

"That doesn't fill me with confidence – I always thought that man was a publicity-seeking charlatan," Leo commented.

"That may be so. I'm sure that dealing with a fringe area like this will uncover a load of attention seekers, those with delusional mental problems and other whack-jobs. Our research appears to focus on two main aspects of the paranormal – clairvoyance and remote viewing. Clairvoyance was the logical one to start with. From what I've read, a clairvoyant is given as much information as possible about a person of interest – for example, details about a Russian nuclear weapons builder. The clairvoyant then tries to link minds with this person and attempts to see what they see and think what they think. Apparently, the Soviets were further ahead and attempting to control their targets' thoughts. However, I couldn't find any examples where they were successful. Trying to get personal details of a target for a clairvoyant to use was difficult, to say the least. This led one group to attempt something extraordinary; they took the person out of the equation. Armed with only an aerial photograph of a region, they would try to build up a picture of what was going on there. Remote viewing was born. I have no idea how this is supposed to work. Some suggest that these remote viewers somehow tap into the collective unconscious. If you are a Star Wars fan, I guess it's the equivalence of The Force. I remember reading that at the time of the 9/11 attacks, highly sensitive random number generators experienced disturbances worldwide. Some say that the collective shock felt by so many affected the very fabric of our universe – our reality." Bob handed a few pages of project notes to Leo.

"All well and good, Bob, but Fairbrother predicted future events," Leo replied as he scanned the pages handed to him.

Bob continued. "It appears precognition was one of the aspects of the paranormal that was also investigated. However, their interest focussed only on near-future events. For example, when would a nuclear sub be ready for launch? Put it into context, Leo. How could Fairbrother or anyone else, for that matter, work out from those squiggles that twenty-odd years into the future, two aircraft would bring down the World Trade Towers, and another would smash into the Pentagon? How would you even know that you were tapping into a future event? That's probably one of the reasons we closed the project down in '95 – there was simply no way to differentiate success from guesswork. In 1995, Fairbrother's work would have been considered meaningless drivel."

"I see what you mean, Bob. However, it looks as if we now have definitive proof that Fairbrother had precognitive skills – not predicting what may happen tomorrow but, if rather cryptically, what will happen decades into the future. We need to pay attention to his work – especially in light of the new material."

Bob Dexter nodded. He'd initially thought that the day would be like any other one. He stood up and poured Leo and himself a fresh coffee from a jug on the credenza. Walking to the window, he took a sip as he gazed into infinity. The aroma of the coffee was calming, and the bitter after-taste was always comforting. "Leo, you realise if this all pans out, we will have one hell of a barn fight on our hands."

"I don't understand," Leo replied.

"Well, it's a jurisdictional nightmare? CIA, DIA, and Army INSCOM have been involved in this project at some time and NASA, the USAF, GSFC, JPL, and not to mention the Whitehouse, Congress, the FBI and damned NSA will have to be involved. How many egos will we have to contain to get this whole shebang to work? Talk about herding cats! Then, look at the cost. It could easily run into the billions. Where is all of that going to come from? And how do we keep this all secret from the public? If this were to leak, it would have the potential to cause chaos. Hell, Leo, I don't know where I should start on this one. Should I push it onto the Director and let him run with it, or should I take this on directly? It may get me out of doing some of the same crappy routine jobs every month – but it's likely to be a career maker or career breaker. I'm too young to retire and too old to slide down the corporate ladder." Bob drained the last of his coffee from his mug and proceeded back to the credenza for a refill.

Leo was beginning to think that Bob had wished he had never come to work that day. He's going to ignore it – bury it, Leo thought. "I would suggest the old softly-softly catchy monkey approach, Bob." Leo said and continued, "I can see several arguments as to why the CIA can maintain control of this situation. I also know where you can source funds – at least enough to get us started without raising eyebrows. There will be plenty of slush funds from my day that are sitting idle and forgotten about – even now. Of course, we would need executive authority to access these. The important thing, Bob, is that the events in Fairbrother's report are starting to happen, and we do not have the luxury of time."

Bob nodded in agreement. "I will have to take this to the Director as soon as possible. He's not going to like it. He focuses most of his time on Iran, Iraq, Afghanistan, and South American drug operations. This one's going to hit him from left field. I'm sure of that."

"In that case, may I suggest you request control over running the show? If allowed, the next step would be to go right to the top – it's that important. However, should anything hit the fan, I'll gladly take the heat and be the fall guy. What's the worst they can do? Sack me?" Leo replied with a snigger.

Bob nodded, running his hand through his hair and gripping the back of his neck. "Leo, keep all of this close to your chest for the time being. The Director is back tomorrow – I'll ask for a priority meeting and will let you know how I get on. If I get to run with this, I would like you to be my 2IC. Somehow, I don't think you will have a problem with that."

Leo simply smiled in return.

"Good," Bob replied. "I'll need some supporting documentation for Preston. I can work back tonight, but can you arrange a brief report to prove to him that I'm not a complete loon?"

"I can have it to you first thing in the morning," Leo responded.

They shook hands, and Leo left the office. It's amazing what a sense of purpose does to a person, Bob concluded as he realised that Leo had much more energy and spring to his step at the end of the meeting compared to the start. I wonder if I will have as much drive when I'm his age – if I'm still around, Bob thought. He sat at his computer, opened a new word-processing document and stared at the empty white page before him. He chewed on a pencil as he wondered how in hell he would explain the situation to the Director.

Laura arrived at work that morning with a strong sense of apprehension. Less than 14 hours earlier, she and Brad had put the finishing touches on the algorithms and routines she would apply to the lunar imagery. At just after 6:00 PM, Laura clicked the button that kicked thousands of computers, located all around the world, into action. She tried to envision each of those computers as snippets of information were sent to them to be processed. Some would be in offices, others in dens and even bedrooms. Many were in the USA, but she was surprised to hear from Brad that some of the volunteer computers were in places such as Iran, China and even North Korea via clandestine proxy servers. Each of these computers on the grid would request a parcel of data, process it, and post the results to a central server within the GSFC.

With her usual flair, Laura energetically flung her handbag under her desk – it made a bigger bang on the partition wall than usual. She switched her monitors on and smiled as she saw the program's progress overnight. Almost 52% of the data had been processed. At this rate, it would take just over a day to process the high-resolution imagery for the entire Moon. She felt the tension literally flow out of her neck and shoulders. She had awoken that morning from a terrible dream in which less than 1% of the data had been processed. A night of twisting and turning had felt like an eternity. Laura's mind had continued to race all night long. All her fears and insecurities had surfaced to haunt her through the darkness. It had felt so real that when she awoke, Laura had to retrace her steps over the past day to reassure herself that it was all just a nasty dream.

Brad visited Laura's cubicle within 10 minutes of her arrival. "I come bearing gifts," he said as he handed Laura a large cup of coffee and a paper bag containing a sugar-dusted lemon-filled doughnut. He sat beside her and stared into his paper bag, "Mmm, the breakfast of champions." Within six bites, he had demolished his doughnut, got fine sugar dust on his shirt and lap, and had a white nose. "How's the process going?" Brad asked as he took a sip of coffee.

"Thanks for breakfast, Brad. I now see why you are so bouncy in the morning with all that sugar you eat." Laura looked up at Brad and stifled a laugh, "Or perhaps it's all the cocaine you're on!"

"Cocaine?" Brad replied with confusion.

Laura tapped her nose, "We're at 52 percent and climbing. All things equal, I think it will be complete by around 8:00 PM tonight."

"Damn, I thought we would have been at around 70% by now," Brad replied as he wiped the tip of his nose and flicked as much sugar as he could from his shirt and trousers. It left little white streaks on his dark grey pants. "If you look in your shared drive, you will see a program I've put there for you. It's my 'slice and show' application. It will take the output data, look for extremes and then display the actual LRO and DEM imagery for areas that match the criteria. A little overview window shows you where you are on the Moon. You just have to hit the space key to rotate between LRO, DEM and merged imagery and the return key to look at the next match. If you find a scene of interest, press the tab key, and the program will flag it for you. It saves you from zooming and panning around the images."

Laura's eyes brightened. "That's fantastic, Brad. I was starting to dread the task of having to scroll over all of that area again."

"You can get through the data quite quickly with my 'slice and show' – it's so good I think I will advertise it on cable TV!" Brad demonstrated the program to Laura and then let her take the controls. Within a few minutes, she had gotten the hang of things. As a first pass, they entered the simplified morphological parameters for the Apollo Lunar Landers. There were just over 6,000 objects comparable in size, shape and aspect in their sample image. Within 30 key presses, she had identified the Apollo 14 landing site close to the lunar equator in the Frau Mauro formation.

"That's the Antares Lunar Module! You can even see the

astronauts' footprints." She pointed out the faint trail leading a hundred or so metres to the module's left. "Brad, you are an absolute genius – not to mention a saint and lifesaver! From now on, I think I will call you Saint Brad!" Laura hugged Brad – and felt a little disappointed when Brad did not reciprocate as warmly as she had expected.

The white van was in the same place as the day before. It was a cold and crisp autumnal morning, and the lone figure sat in the back, vigorously rubbing his hands together for warmth. His nose was running – he knew he had a cold coming. However, nothing was going to stop him. Not now. He wiped his nose with the back of his hand and listened intently to the conversation between Laura and Brad. He scribbled into his notepad as he sniffed and snorted. Now and then, he would take a swig from a bottle of cheap whisky hidden within a crumpled brown paper bag. The liquor was raw and burnt his throat – but it gave him warmth. It was almost a new Moon – the time was coming, he thought. I must be ready; I must be prepared.

Laura looked at her watch – it was 1:20 PM and well into her lunch break. The progress bar for the BOINC program hovered around the 60 per cent completed mark. She had not left her cubicle all day, and since Brad had left, she had manually examined well over a thousand matches identified by the neural networks they had set up. With only a few keys to control the software and with no need to flick between keyboard and mouse, Laura had found Brad's 'slice-and-show' program quick and easy to use. She was currently assessing the data for objects that are most geometrically perfect – squares, rectangles and the like.

As she hit the return key, she froze as she saw the image before her. A nearly perfect rectangle aligned about 30 degrees east from lunar north along its long axis. She looked at the scale of the photo – the feature was a good 10m x 60m in size. Due to the lack of an atmosphere, the lunar daylight is harsh, and shadows are crisp and black. Laura could work out from the shadows that this feature had height – it wasn't a glitch on the sensor. However, the shadowing didn't look entirely right to her – light seemed to pass through the object, making the shadow look like an elongated pair of dark black trousers. Laura quickly pressed the tab key to flag its location, and not taking any chances, she jotted down the coordinates as well. She hit the return key to display the next match and gasped when she saw an almost identical object on the screen. It must be a problem with the imagery, Laura thought. Then she looked closer. This feature, which appeared similar in size to the other, was oriented at a slightly different angle. Again she hit the tab key and noted the coordinates. That's strange, Laura thought, as she realised that the two features were close to one another, just on the far side, relatively close to the lunar North Pole. Because of their proximity, Laura hit the 'minus' key several times to zoom out. She saw a flat crater, several hundred metres or so in diameter. However, when zooming into the crater's edge, Laura could see that it was rimmed by many similar rectangular blocks. Laura felt her heart beat faster and harder than usual and started to feel a little light-headed. This can't be natural, she thought, is Brad screwing with me? Not wanting to change what was on the screen, Laura picked up the phone and dialled Brad's cubicle. He answered almost immediately.

"Hi, LM. Are you offering to buy me a late lunch?" Brad asked.

"Not just yet, Brad. Please don't take this the wrong way, but did you mess with the LRO imagery in any way?"

"No, why would I do that?"

"You have a bit of a reputation as a prankster – admit it," Laura said.

"I saw the errors in my ways, LM. Seriously, cross my heart and all that. I have not messed around with your data."

Laura could hear the seriousness in Brad's voice. "You'll want to come here and see this." She hung up without allowing Brad to reply and turned her attention back to the computer screen.

Within a few seconds, Brad arrived at Laura's cubicle. "So, what have you found?" Although he had only jogged some 15 metres from his desk, Brad sounded a little out of breath.

"Take a look," Laura responded and pointed at two images on her screen. "This crater is rimmed with these smaller objects."

Brad sat down and brought his face so close to the screen that his nose almost touched it. "Wow, that's interesting. Any idea what it is?" Brad queried.

"None at all. I can't even guess what sort of process could turn a crater rim into those blocks," replied Laura. "They are all the same size, as far as I can tell."

"But what's with the shadowing? It looks vaguely familiar. Laura, open up a browser for me."

Laura started a new browser, and a Google search box appeared. Brad typed so fast that Laura could only make out the last few words 'from the air'. Within a second, a whole heap of image thumbs appeared. Brad quickly scanned them and clicked on the one he thought most appropriate. A page from the science and technology section of MSNBC's website appeared. "Look familiar?" Brad asked. "Look at the shadowing."

Laura stared in disbelief. Brad was right. The strange trouser-like shadows could be explained – was explained – by looking at an image of Stonehenge from the air. "They're standing stones!" Laura gasped.

"Whoa, girl, hold your horses. I don't know what they are, just that the shadowing is reminiscent of Stonehenge. I was there only last year. It's a really eerie place, especially in the morning mist. Whatever it is, we need higher resolution data to look at and imagery with a lower sun angle." Brad replied.

"Where are we going to get that from?"

"No idea, LM, but I think you may have found what the suits were after. I'd let Simmons know about this as soon as you can." Brad replied and glanced at his watch. "Crap, I'm late for a meeting and got to go, but please keep me in the loop on this... whatever it is." Brad patted Laura on the shoulder and headed off.

Laura stared at the images on her screen for a bit longer. She felt comforted that she had found something of interest to report. Laura then picked up the phone and called Simmons' secretary. He was not in the office that day, but Laura managed to schedule a meeting first thing the following morning. Slightly disappointed that she couldn't get to see him right away, she appreciated the fact that it gave her ample time to arrange a presentation.

In the white van, two red-rimmed and blood-shot eyes stared into infinity. The bottle of whisky was empty, and the lone figure sat with the headset pressed to his ear as he dragged on a cigarette. His eyes widened as he listened to the conversation between Laura and Brad. His hands started to tremble, and he could feel his heart race. He took another long drag and stamped out the half-finished cigarette on the van's wall. He leaned his head back and blew the smoke towards the ceiling. A smile formed on his thin lips, and then he jolted upright. No time to lose; I must be on the ball, he thought. 'History will be made today!' he wrote in his notepad with shaking hands.

Laura had spent all of the afternoon staring at the images of the strange crater near the lunar North Pole. She had just about completed a slideshow presentation that outlined her task and methodology, as well as a selection of images of the feature, which she had called the Anomalous Lunar Feature Number 1, or ALF-1. I must check to see if there are any other similar features, she thought. Laura opened the BOINC program on her computer and saw that the dataset processing was at 89%. She looked at her watch – 8:15 PM – and realised it would take several more hours to complete. Early night again, Laura thought as she saved her presentation and printed a few copies. She reached under her desk and groped around for her bag. She did not notice the small black box which had fallen onto the floor from under her desk. Laura switched off her monitors and headed for the printer. Before heading to the elevator, she made a brief detour to drop a copy of the presentation on Brad's desk.

It was an especially dark and cold evening as Laura made her way across the car park. Laura had trouble finding her keys with the presentation rolled up in her bag. So much for remotes, she mused. She had already reached her car and had not yet located her keys. Laura placed her purse on the roof and began to fumble around inside. Out of the corner of her eye, something grabbed her attention. She looked up and saw a hint of an aurora Borealis high in the sky. Pastel greens, yellows, oranges and even whispers of reds flickered in the night sky as the solar winds channelled by Earth's magnetic field were discharged in the upper atmosphere as they spiralled down towards the ground.

The sky show made for a perfect distraction. Laura never noticed the man that approached her from behind. She managed a barely audible snuffle as the gloved hand cupped a chloroform-soaked rag over her nose and mouth. Laura gasped for breath as she struggled to break free. Her eyes rolled upwards, her vision blackened, and her body went limp as she drifted off into unconsciousness.

## Chapter Twelve

Brad Sommers eyed himself in the mirror-walled elevator and smiled approvingly at his reflection as he tousled his hair to perfection. As soon as the doors opened, he made his way to Laura's cubicle but was disappointed to find it vacant. With a shrug of his shoulders, he headed to his desk and was happy to see a copy of her presentation resting on his keyboard. Brad sat down and started to read. It was a good presentation – concise, well organised and careful to exclude any supposition. It was not until he had finished reading it that he noticed the message light on his phone blinking. He hit the message retrieval button and heard the voice of Simmons' secretary. Laura had not turned up for her 8:00 AM meeting, and no one knew where she was. Brad glanced at his watch – almost 9:30 AM. This is not like her, he thought. He rang her cell phone, but it went straight through to voicemail. He checked his cell phone but there were no calls from her. Brad returned to Laura's station – perhaps she had left him a note. When he reached her desk, there was a sticky note with a message, but it was not from her. 'Found this under your desk – think you must have lost it – R.' The message was from Raul, one of the janitors. Brad looked at the little black box to which the note was attached. His brow furrowed as he examined the device. It contained no markings, just a few micro switches, a battery cover, a few little holes and a single black wire hanging out of it. On one side was a strip of Velcro. He reread the note – 'Found under the desk,' he muttered to himself. Brad got down on his hands and knees and felt around underneath the desk. It didn't take long to locate the other half of the Velcro. It's a damn bug, he realised. He was about to open it to pull the battery out but thought better of it. Someone may still be listening on the other end, he thought. If I turn it off, they will know that the bug, if that is what it is, has been discovered. Instead, he placed the device on the table and jogged back to his cubicle. He got down on all fours and checked under his desk – nothing there. Whilst still on his knees, he grappled for his phone, called Simmons' secretary and told her of his discovery and fears.

Laura was confused and terrified when she awoke. Still groggy, she managed to position herself into a sitting position in the back of the van – no easy feat considering that her hands were tied behind her back with nylon restraints and her ankles bound together with duct tape. A piece of tape also covered her mouth. She looked around and tried to focus. It was very dark inside the van, but from light entering through scratches on a painted-out window and from a ceiling vent, she could tell it was light outside. I've been out for hours, she thought. She took some deep breaths, and the mind fug induced by the chloroform began to fade; she became more aware of her surroundings. The air in the van was pungent – all she could smell was a combination of smoke, sweat, urine and liquor. She could also feel the van moving. It didn't feel like it was going fast, and the ride was smooth. We're in the suburbs, she surmised.

Suddenly the van stopped – the engine left running. Laura could hear the driver getting out, followed by footsteps and a low rumbling sound. The driver got back into his seat and edged the van forward. They stopped again within seconds, and she felt the shudder as the engine switched off. Laura could hear the driver exit the van and the same low rumbling sound. It's a roller door, she realised, and I'm in some kind of warehouse. She shuffled herself around so that her knees were bent and her feet were touching the seam between the rear doors. Laura's heart began to pound as she heard the footsteps approach, clicking on a concrete floor. She heard the latch on the door turn. As soon as the door opened, she pressed her hands to the floor behind her and kicked out with all her might. Laura heard a thud as her abductor was thrown backwards and hit the ground hard. He gave out a muffled groan. A futile act, Laura knew, as there was nothing else for her to do. With her arms and legs bound as they were, she had no hope of escape. She drew her knees to her chest again in preparation for another attack.

The man was unprepared for her assault. The door had hit him hard in the head, and the force of the blow had thrown him several feet backwards onto the dusty and uneven concrete floor. He got back to his feet and dusted himself off as he moved back towards the van – more cautiously this time. He could see the fear in her eyes and her determination to defend herself, and she could kick like a mule. He stood out of range of her feet and stared silently into Laura's dark, angry eyes.

Laura felt as if the man's stare was burning a hole through her eyes and into the back of her head. He looked vaguely familiar. His eyes were a piercing blue that contrasted against the raw red lids. His stubbled, gaunt and emotionless face betrayed no hint of his intentions. Laura glanced up and down and noticed the dirty clothes he was wearing. He looked like a tramp – quite literally. Over a well-worn pair of jeans and a moth-eaten sweatshirt, he wore a sweat-stained beige trench coat tied loosely around his waist. He wore an old pair of badly frayed sandshoes. He's no professional, she thought. He's not hiding his face – he doesn't care if I can identify him! She felt a lump form in her throat, and thoughts of rape and torture flashed through Laura's mind. The abductor had no fear of the consequences of his actions. She was going to die.

Within a few minutes of making his call, Brad was in Simmons' office, pacing up and down. "I can't be a hundred percent sure, Boss, but the thing velcroed under Laura's desk looks like a bug to me."

Simmons clicked the intercom on his phone, "Tina, Laura's absence may have taken a sinister turn. Could you please call the FBI and get someone down here ASAP? Tell them it involves possible espionage and abduction." He turned his attention to Brad, "Do you think Laura planted the bug? Do you think she could be complicit in her own disappearance?"

"No way, Boss," Brad replied, "The bug was found on the floor by Raul, the janitor and placed on her desk this morning. Boss, Laura made a discovery in the LRO data yesterday and worked back late to get a presentation ready for you." Brad handed his copy of the presentation over to Simmons.

Simmons flicked through the report and could see the information of importance within it, but his mind could not focus on the content. "Brad, the FBI should be here soon. I'll keep you posted on events. Don't inform anyone else about the bug – I don't want anyone outside to overhear anything that could jeopardise Laura's safety. If she was abducted, that is."

Realising the meeting was over, Brad nodded in acknowledgement and left the office. Simmons fell into his chair and reviewed her presentation. She had found something of interest. Was it a coincidence that she went missing the very same day of her discovery? Simmons mulled over that thought for a while, then pressed the intercom button again, "Tina, please get me Leo Helfgott on the line ASAP. If he's busy, tell him it's urgent."

Within a minute, Tina had patched Neil through to Leo.

Simmons spent no time on formalities, "Leo, we have a bit of a situation here. Laura Meadows has gone missing, and it looks like a bug was secreted under her desk. Her disappearance happened on the day she made a discovery in the LRO imagery. Are any of your spooks at the CIA involved in this?"

"A discovery?" Leo responded, and then realising that someone's life was potentially in jeopardy, changed the topic, "No, no, no, the bug has nothing to do with me. Do you want me to arrange for some CIA reps to come down?"

"That's not necessary, Leo. I've called the FBI, and I'm sure they will be here soon. Anyway, I think you need to come in and see the report that Laura completed before she went missing. I haven't had time to digest it, but I think you will find it interesting."

"I'll be there within the hour. Best of luck in finding Laura."

Simmons hung up the phone. He returned his attention to the report and noticed the timestamp at the bottom of the cover page – 11/3/10 20:16. He hit the intercom button, "Tina, find out what parking space Laura has allocated and see if her vehicle is still there. Also, Laura used the printer around 8:16 PM last night. Can you check the printer logs and see when she last used the machine? Take that information to security and get copies of all cameras that lead from her station to her car parking spot. I want to build a picture of what happened as she left the office last night. I would like all of this ready for the FBI when they get here."

Under the dim emergency lighting, FBI Special Agent Michael Robinson sat at Laura's desk and carefully examined the device in his latex-gloved hands. At least two people had handled it since it was placed, which significantly diminished the chances of pulling any decent prints of the bug – if there were any.

Special Agent Robinson knew that many modern bugging devices use the same frequencies as mobile phones, making them more challenging to detect. On his arrival at the GSFC just ten minutes earlier, he had requested that power to the building be cut. This had two benefits – first, it significantly reduced the number and intensity of electrical signals and noise in the air, and second, it provided an excellent reason to get everyone else, along with their mobile phones, out of the area.

Robinson felt a tap on the shoulder from colleague Angela Dawson, one of the FBI's best technical specialists. She pointed to the equipment she had set up on the desk and gave him a thumbs-up signal. The device was a sophisticated bug sweeper and electronic countermeasures suite capable of scanning millions of frequencies simultaneously. A single unit can analyse for unusual radio activity, and a pair of them could accurately pinpoint any bugging devices to within a few metres. Michael carefully placed the bug back on the desk, and they both stared at the display on the bug sweeper – there was very little activity on the screen. Dawson wrote some words on her notepad and showed it to Robinson – 'no activity – battery dead or voice-activated / burst tx'. Special Agent Robinson nodded and pointed to the iPod in Dawson's kit. She connected it to a small pair of speakers and selected an audio file from the menu. She hit the play button, and two female voices could be heard talking on some mundane topic about men, sports and testosterone. Twenty seconds passed when a flash of activity appeared on the bug sweeper screen. It lasted a fraction of a second, but it was enough to capture useful information such as frequency and signal strength. Angela passed another note under Special Agent Robinson's nose – 'voice-activated burst transmitter 2.4GHz max range 800m'. Robinson nodded and replied with a 'let's go' hand signal. Dawson slowly turned the volume of the iPod down so it would sound as if the two people had walked out of earshot. They both headed for Simmons' office.

Leo had arrived shortly after the FBI had started their work. He sat in Simmons' office and read through Laura's report.

"Is this the sort of thing you have been looking for?" Simmons asked.

"Quite possibly," Leo replied. "The project I am involved in is quite unusual, to say the least. I wish I could tell you more at this stage. However, based on this report, I think I will need to talk to the committee and see if we can bring you into the fold."

"I would appreciate that, Leo," Simmons responded. He was a little shocked when he heard the word 'committee'. It sounded like he was a pawn in a much larger project than he had imagined.

There was a knock on the door and Special Agents Robinson and Dawson entered. Robinson looked at Leo and then back at Neil.

"It's alright, Special Agent Robinson, he's from the..."

"I'm just an old friend. Call me Leo." Leo cut in.

"We have a bugging device and a moderately sophisticated one. It's a voice-activated burst transmitter. It means that it records audio only when voices are heard. It stores several seconds of voice then transmits it at great speed – in a burst – to whoever is listening." Robinson explained.

"What agency could do this sort of thing?" Simmons asked.

"The device is not that sophisticated – nowadays you can pick these things up for a few hundred bucks on the Internet – anyway, the placement of the bug hints at amateurism. If anything, I would say that it was placed there by someone who works here. Did she have any workplace romances go sour?" The agent asked.

"How long has the device been there?" Leo asked, ignoring his question.

"It's hard to say. As I said, it's a voice-activated burst transmitter. That alone means that it is very energy efficient. It's still working, so, to hazard a guess, it could have been there for days – maybe even a few weeks. I will be able to tell you more once we get it back to the lab."

"Up to six weeks," Dawson interjected. She had been accessing the Internet on her phone. "It's an X-111 single-channel burst transmitter and is available on i-spy-u.com for three hundred and ninety-nine dollars plus tax." She held up an image of the device on her phone. It was identical to the one on Laura's desk.

"Where do we go from here?" Simmons asked.

"We know the specifications of the transmitter used, and we know its range limitations. We have detection gear in our truck, and we'll sweep the perimeter looking for a receiver locked into that same frequency."

There was another knock on the door.

"Come," Simmons said out loud.

Tina came in holding a DVD and looking quite pale. She passed the disk to Simmons. "This is the security camera footage you asked for, sir. I haven't seen it as the power is still off, but security says it shows Laura being abducted from the car park at 8:22 PM last night. It's all on camera 021."

The room was silent. Simmons inserted the disc into his notebook computer and double-clicked on the icon representing the video for that particular security camera. The FBI agents gathered around behind Simmons. Leo stayed where he was and motioned for Tina to sit next to him. She was almost in tears. Leo placed his hand on her shoulder for comfort.

The screen displayed a wide-angle view of the car park from a fixed CCTV camera. The car park was almost deserted, with Laura's car to the right of the screen and a few pool cars in the middle of the frame. Part of a white van was visible to the left. They watched as the figure of Laura walked to her car. She waited at her car for a while, but the imagery was too grainy to see what she was doing. Quite quickly, a figure approached her from behind, grabbed her, and a brief struggle ensued. Simmons gasped as the assailant dragged Laura's limp and unconscious body towards the white van. He looked over at Tina with concerned eyes – it was enough to make her cry.

"Angela, call HQ and tell them we have an abduction situation. Take a copy of the security vision for analysis – we need a tag number on that white van. Also, do a perimeter sweep and see if we can find the listening post. My guess is that it is in that vehicle, but we need to make sure." Special Agent Robinson ordered. He focused on Tina and continued, "We'll go all-out to get Laura back. This guy is an amateur and probably working alone. That makes our life a lot easier." The agent turned back to Simmons. "We'll be heading to our vehicle now. It's got a counter surveillance suite and computer gear that will allow us to analyse the camera footage. Once we have done our sweep, I'll take the listening device with us. I may have something for you in an hour or so. If you have any further information, then please let me know. You can restore power to the building once we've left." He handed out his business card to Neil, Tina and Leo. Simmons ejected the DVD and handed it over to Robinson. Angela Dawson was still on the phone with FBI headquarters and acknowledged the end of the meeting with a little wave of her free hand as they both left the office.

The two agents got into the back of their vehicle – a large white van with no markings. Outwardly, it looked much like the van used by the abductor, except it was much newer. However, on the inside, it was a different beast entirely. Inside, the FBI vehicle wouldn't look out of place as the bridge of a spaceship – albeit a compact one. It was a tech-head's wet dream. One wall of the van had a narrow bench into which three keyboards were embedded. The wall behind the bench contained flat-panel computer displays and other electronic gear – each perfectly suited to its designated task.

Agent Dawson sat at her station and linked the surveillance equipment in the van via radio to the portable surveillance suite, which still sat at Laura's desk. The two units were now connected and working as a pair. Through triangulation, she could pinpoint any receiver within a couple of kilometres that was tuned into the same frequency as the listening device. She keyed in the bug's frequency and clicked on the icon marked 'Scan'. Within the portable device on Laura's desk and in a small dome on the van's roof, tiny but highly sensitive directional antennae rotated. A new display appeared on her screen. It showed the radio spectrum from medium wave through to gigahertz satellite frequencies. Through a snowfield of dots, lines became visible that indicated active receivers and transmitters. As the antennae rotated, lines would disappear, and new ones would appear. With a couple of clicks of the mouse, Dawson configured the display to show only the frequency range used by the listening device. With the office evacuated, there was nothing for the bug to capture, so it transmitted nothing. Dawson's display showed nothing but static. There was no listening device within range of their van. She turned to Robinson. "It looks as if you are right, Mike, nothing but static on the scanner."

The agent gave a small grunt in acknowledgement. He was sitting at the neighbouring workstation and was perusing the security camera footage. "Got you, you bastard!" he muttered under his breath. Dawson looked over to see an image of the van from a shallower angle. Agent Robinson had managed to zoom in and, with a bit of image processing, made out the licence plate. He opened a browser window and connected to the FBI's secure network. Within seconds he had a whole page of information in front of him. The tags matched the vehicle, which hadn't been reported as lost or stolen. "I think we are in luck, Angela. Our purp' has been careless. I'll get a team over to his last known place of residence. Let's go back and see if Simmons knows anything about this guy."

Tina was at a filing cabinet trying to focus on work when Special Agent Robinson entered. She wasn't having much success. "Have you found something?" she asked, expecting to hear bad news.

"We already have a name, and agents are on their way to his house as we speak. Could you pass this through HR and see if he is or was associated with the facility." Agent Robinson handed Tina a piece of paper with a name on it. "OK to go in?" he asked with a hopeful look.

Tina managed a weak smile and escorted him into Simmons' office. She held his note up, "I'll be right on it."

"That's quick. Have you got something already?" Simmons asked.

"It looks as if the abductor is an amateur. We've got a name, and Tina is checking with Human Resources to see if there is a connection with your facility. He handed a printout of a driver's licence to Neil. "This is the owner of the van, which hasn't been reported lost or stolen, so we are assuming at this stage that this is our guy. Does he look familiar to you?"

Neil shook his head. "No, I've never seen him before, but this is a large facility, and there are so many workers I never even see. Who is this Peter Fairbrother anyway? Is he dangerous?"

A chill ran down Leo's spine as he heard the name. He kept quiet.

"He's a nobody. I've looked at his RAP sheet, and he's had several run-ins with the law – mainly for disturbing the peace – but nothing of this magnitude. He's been in and out of psychiatric hospitals many times due to his misdemeanours and was last released just six months ago. Currently, he has no outstanding warrants. I initiated a bureau-wide BOLO just before I came back. Agent Dawson will be putting out an inter-agency one soon, if not already. Every law enforcement agency and school crossing guard will be on the lookout for this guy and his van. We'll also be going through whatever CCTV we can get our hands on to see if we can track where he went." Robinson retrieved the printout of Peter Fairbrother's driving license from Simmons. And, as if flicking the switch himself, just as Special Agent Robinson took hold of the paper, the power to the office was suddenly restored. Everyone in the room looked up at the lights as they came back on. "I guess that's our cue to get down to business. I'll be in touch as soon as I have any news." Robinson shook hands with Simmons and Leo and left the office.

With some effort, Leo managed to extricate himself from the chair. "It's been an extraordinary start to the day, Neil. I do hope that Laura comes out of this both safe and well. Is it OK if I take this report with me?"

"Sure, just get Tina to run me off a copy. Leo, what are the chances that this abduction has something to do with Laura's work and that report?"

"That, I simply do not know." Leo lied with a shrug of his shoulders. Leo had never heard of Peter Fairbrother, but it was surely beyond coincidence that an unrelated person with the same surname would become involved. "I must get back to my office. Please let me know if there are any developments." They shook hands, and Leo left.

Sitting alone in his office, Simmons mentally reviewed the morning's developments. He had noticed Leo's uneasiness at the mention of the name of the alleged abductor. He's hiding something, he thought to himself.

Peter Fairbrother had been more cautious the second time he went to the back of the van. Laura was like a scorpion poised for an attack; whenever he got close, she lashed out with her bound but powerful legs. After several more kicks, one on the solar plexus and the other dangerously near the head, Peter realised he could effectively use one of the van's doors as a shield. He kept the door between himself and Laura and grabbed her bound ankles with his free hand. Jerking hard, Laura lost her balance and hit her head on the van floor. He tugged hard, and she fell out of the van, landing on her coccyx. The pain was excruciating as the shockwave rode up her spine. Blissful unconsciousness replaced the pain as the back of her head struck the van's towbar. A trickle of blood stained the concrete on which she lay.

# Chapter Thirteen

It was early afternoon, and Leo Helfgott and Bob Dexter stood at the drinks machine in the CIA cafeteria. Bob flicked through his spare change, looking for a quarter. Having found one, he promptly purchased a soda and walked with Leo to the most secluded corner he could find. Although a high-traffic area, the cafeteria was routinely swept for listening devices and had been set up to allow veiled discussion without fear of being overheard.

Leo relayed the salient points of his morning to Bob and handed over a copy of Laura's report.

"Peter Fairbrother, you say?" Bob asked as he flicked through the report.

"That's correct, Bob. I did a check as soon as I got back to the office. He's Richard Fairbrother's son and is Lisa's older brother."

"What are the odds?" Bob replied, waving the report in his hand. "You know as well as I that, as a spook, you learn not to believe in coincidences. Now we have a dead soothsayer, his deranged son, who has been bugging the person who has discovered something unusual on the Moon – something that the dead guy predicted. What do you make of all this?" He dropped the report onto the table.

"Well, I think we can conclude that there is something to this pre-cognition thing. What if it's genetic? What if Peter has some of his father's abilities and cannot understand them? What I do know is that we must tell the FBI anything we can to aid Laura's safe return. I also believe that the GSFC head, Neil Simmons, needs full disclosure. We'll need to take a closer look at that... whatever it is, and he will be indispensable for that." Leo said, slapping the back of his hand on the image of ALF-1 in Laura's report.

"I agree, Leo. Let's arrange to meet Simmons as soon as possible.

I'm sure the FBI is already checking Peter's relations, but contact them anyway and let them know of a potential relationship between the abduction and a classified project of national importance. Stress that it has nothing to do with terrorism – say it's related to industrial espionage. We don't want them wasting time running down dead ends." He picked up the report and leafed through it again. "I'm not sure what we have achieved so far, but at least we have a name for our project. How does Project Moonshadow sound?" Bob drained the final few drops of the soda from the can.

"I'll get onto the FBI and see how soon we can meet Simmons. As for the project name – I like it. But I thought the CIA had a special department for coming up with these?" Leo ended jokingly.

"Now, that is a secret reserved only for the Director himself." Bob crumpled the can and helped Leo out of his chair. "Leo, I'll arrange for any info we have on Peter Fairbrother to be sent to you to pass on to the FBI. Let's see if we can meet with Simmons – today if possible. I have no problems going to the GSFC. With a person down, I wouldn't want to go off-site if I was in his position."

Simmons stared at the clock on his wall – it was almost 16:00. He glanced at his watch, hoping to see that it was actually earlier – it wasn't. The day had dragged on second by second. With every tick of the clock, he felt that Laura's fate was edging ever closer to being sealed – if it wasn't already. Tina had managed to calm down and had occupied herself doing some mindless but time-consuming tasks that one always finds a reason not to do. He knew she was sitting outside with piles of folders on her desk, sorting, collating, archiving and preening the filing system. He picked up Special Agent Robinson's card from the desk and proceeded to dial the number. Robinson answered almost immediately, and in under a minute, Simmons had received a status report. Peter Fairbrother has no fixed abode, and the address was for his sister, who agents were currently interviewing. The next line of enquiry was to focus on Peter's employment history – where he worked and who he worked with – to see if it would help to track him down. Special Agent Robinson relayed that this approach, along with an analysis of traffic cameras, was the most likely to result in Laura's successful rescue. Still, as with all abduction cases, time was of the essence.

Laura's head was bursting with pain as she regained consciousness. She couldn't remember where she was or how she got there for a moment. Still, it soon returned to her... going to her car... the sickly-sweet overpowering smell of the chloroform-soaked rag... the smelly mad man with the wild piercing blue eyes... kicking the bastard with all her might... being dragged feet first out of the vehicle... then nothing. She tried to open her eyes. Even in the relative darkness of the room, her eyes burnt as she tried to open them. Everything was a blur, and it took several seconds for things to come into focus. Gingerly she lifted her head to see where she was. Her neck was stiff, and the headache increased in intensity a level or two – at least an 8 out of 10. Laura was lying on a camp stretcher underneath an old, musty army-issue blanket. As her hands and arms were unbound, she ran her fingers over the back of her head, which was wrapped in a bandage. Through it, she could feel a sizable bump at the base of her skull. It stung to the touch and made her head throb even worse. She looked at her wristwatch. It took some straining, but she could just make out the time from the luminous glow from the dial – a little after 7 PM. If only she knew what day it was.

There are times in your life when you have an uneasy feeling based on nothing in particular. Laura was experiencing one of those moments. As the goose bumps grew on Laura's arms and the hairs stood up on the nape of her neck, she realised that she wasn't alone – she was being watched. The light in the room was poor, and it took a while before she could make out the lone figure sitting in the corner. Seeing Laura move, the man edged forward out of his seat and started to hum a tune that was familiar to her, but she couldn't put a name to it. Her body tensed as he moved toward her and stared at her with a reptilian gaze.

"I'm sorry for hurting you earlier, but it wasn't my fault. I am your guardian angel and here to protect you – to prepare you." He seemed much calmer and more coherent at the moment, but the intense stare from his bloodshot eyes reminded Laura of how dangerous this person could potentially be.

"Why did you abduct me?" Laura only managed a barely audible croak as her throat was dry and sore.

"Because you are not ready for what lies ahead," he replied.

"I don't understand."

"You have been chosen... you ARE the chosen." the last few words he almost breathed out.

"Chosen for what?" she asked.

He looked puzzled. "You really don't know, do you? I thought you would have some clue. Laura, you are about to become the most important person in the history of the world."

A flood of thoughts went through her head. He knew her name. How did he know this? He could have gone through her things. He was clearly getting agitated, and she had to keep him calm. Her life may depend on it. "You need to explain what's going on."

He looked up, searching for the right words. "It's hard to explain, but you are destined for great things, Laura. You need to believe me. But there are dangers ahead, and I need to prepare you. You must be ready for what is to happen."

"How can I believe someone who kidnapped me!" she responded sharply, ignoring the advice she gave herself.

He was getting stressed. "There was no other way. I tried to make conversation with you a few weeks ago, but you were not interested in talking to me."

She searched her memory and made the connection after a few seconds. "You're the janitor that vacuumed the floors each night. I didn't recognise you!" She recalled that he was a bit quirky – she thought he was mildly autistic – and he had tried a few times to start a conversation, but always when she was busy working on a problem.

Like a switch being flicked, the man calmed down, and his voice softened. "Yes, that was me. Now you must listen to me as time is short. You must remember what I am about to tell you, and after we are done, you are free to go. Are you OK with that?"

Not believing a word he said, Laura just nodded and listened – without paying too much attention to what was said, instead thinking of ways to escape.

It was nearly 7:00 PM, and Simmons remained sternly silent as he listened to Bob Dexter and Leo Helfgott recap the events that had culminated with Laura's abduction. The story to him sounded part fantastical and part absurd; he could imagine how Alice felt when she tumbled down the rabbit hole.

"I thought you were hiding something from me about the identity of the abductor Leo." Simmons glared at the old man.

"This project is classified, and I couldn't give you any details when the FBI agent mentioned his name. I didn't even know that this person existed. However, rest assured we provided the FBI with all information we have that could track down his whereabouts." Leo replied, his body language conciliatory.

Simmons flicked through the briefing documents that Bob had handed him once the security clearance formalities had been completed. He shook his head in disbelief as he digested its contents.

"Are you telling me that this Fairbrother guy predicted 9/11, the Challenger and Columbia tragedies years before they happened and that his son has abducted one of my best analysts? It sounds crazy!" Simmons said.

"I was in as much disbelief as you are now when Leo first came to me," Dexter responded. However, with Laura's discovery of the feature on the Moon, we have established a definite point in the notes that Richard Fairbrother produced. Neither Leo nor I could find anything in the notes that mentions Laura's abduction, but there are hints that she will be involved further down the track, so although this may sound absurd, we believe that she will be OK. However, this reference point marked by Laura's discovery tells us that China will attempt to send a manned mission to the Moon within a year or two – some eight years ahead of their original schedule. All indications are that they will get to the whatever-it-is before us. We can't let them do that, yet we are powerless and have no hope of getting there first. The best we can do at the moment is to re-task the LRO to take a closer look at the target – and not much more. Right after this meeting, I will need to convene an emergency meeting of the Moonshadow Committee, including you, Neil. I'm going to suggest that the Vice President put a motion to the President and the Chiefs of Staff to get us back to the lunar surface ASAP to examine the feature. God only knows how we can do that, though. Our shuttle fleet will be retired within six months and with that goes the only way we can get people into low Earth orbit, let alone the additional quarter of million miles to the Moon and back again."

The phone on Simmons' desk rang. He grabbed the phone and listened intently to the person at the other end. Less than a minute later, he hung up without saying a word. "Gentleman, that was Special Agent Robinson with an update for us. It appears they've made some headway and know of a workshop owned by the Fairbrother family, to which Peter Fairbrother has access. They are hopeful that they will find Laura and her abductor there. They expect to be on-site within the hour."

Bob looked at his watch. "I hope they find Laura safe and well. I need to take my leave and arrange the meeting of the Committee. Leo, do you want to come with me or stay here?"

Leo indicated his wish to stay at the GSFC and said to Dexter he would call as soon as he heard from the FBI. With that, Bob left the office. Leo sat with Neil and went through some of the finer aspects of the reports.

# Chapter Fifteen

Special Agent Robinson was in the lead car – a nondescript black sedan. Behind them was an equally innocuous black truck with five FBI tactical specialists in the back. Both vehicles killed their lights just around the corner of the warehouse and came to a slow and silent stop. Robinson tapped his earpiece and ordered the troops to take their positions. Exiting the car with his gun drawn and held low, Special Agent Robinson quietly moved toward the warehouse, checking his surroundings as he went. The warehouse windows were whitewashed over, making it impossible to see into the building. At the main entrance, one of the troops inserted a tiny inspection camera into a small gap between the roller door and the ground. Rotating the articulated tubing, the troop observed the warehouse's interior on a small green-screen monitor. He gave the thumbs up when he recognised the van and two people inside. On seeing the signal, Special Agent Robinson used sign language to direct the troops to get into position, covering the main exits and preparing for a full-frontal assault. Troops placed shaped charges onto the roller door and attached a radio trigger. At one of the obscured windows, another troop stood in position with something that looked like a hammer with an oversized head.

With everybody in position, Special Agent Robinson gave the signal to proceed. The man at the window lifted a missile switch cover on the handle of the "hammer" and flicked the switch underneath – a small red light illuminated. Even though he was wearing goggles, he turned his head as he smashed the hammer into the window. Instantly two things occurred – a flash grenade flew from the head of the hammer into the warehouse and ignited before it hit the ground, and simultaneously it triggered the shaped charge on the roller door. Equipped with goggles and breathing apparatus, two troops carrying P90s and Special Agent

Robinson with his Heckler and Koch drawn and off safety entered the warehouse, ready for action. The intense flash and noise from the explosion disoriented both Laura and Peter. Through watery eyes, Laura could barely make out the troops approaching them but knew they would be ready to shoot. She shouted a "No" as she dived onto Peter to shield him from the approaching soldiers. Within seconds she felt a strong pair of hands drag her off. One of Peter Fairbrother's hands was in the pocket of his trench coat as Laura was being dragged away. He withdrew his hand – he was holding something. In the fraction of a second available to him, the trooper evaluated the situation, saw a threat of a possible explosive device and fired two rounds in quick succession from his P90 into Fairbrother's head at point-blank range. He died instantly. His hand fell open to reveal a small black notebook.

Simmons hung up the phone and quickly made his way to the door. Popping his head around the door, he called out to Tina. "Good news Tina, Laura's been rescued! She's safe and well and is on her way to the hospital for a check-up. Could you let Brad know, then take yourself home? I don't expect to see you here tomorrow." He could hear Tina crying with relief as she placed a call to Brad.

Leo had heard the conversation and felt like a great weight had lifted from his shoulders, knowing that Laura was safe. "Good news that Laura is OK. Is there any news on Peter Fairbrother? When do you think we could speak with him?" Leo asked in rapid succession.

"Never," Simmons replied, "they thought he had an explosive on him and put a round into his head."

From elation to deflation, Leo told Simmons, "He might have been able to tell us so much... possibly explain some of his father's notes... now we will never know."

Simmons nodded, "The FBI is going through his effects. Apparently, there is a load of notebooks and tapes in his van. Perhaps these will provide us with some answers. Christ, this must be the weirdest freaking day of my life, but I think stranger things may lie ahead." He pulled the bottle of single malt Scotch whisky out of his drawer and poured Leo and himself each a generous measure.

# Chapter Sixteen

Laura was groggy when she awoke – her whole body felt numb. It was a strangely reassuring feeling, especially considering the crack to the skull that she had received.

She breathed in deeply – all she could smell was clinical disinfectant. She looked at her hands and noticed the intravenous line that entered her left forearm. She was in a hospital. Laura gave out a sigh of relief at the realisation she was safe.

Her mouth was dry, and her lips felt like they were about to crack. She managed to reach out and press the yellow call button with some effort. Within a minute, a nurse arrived at her bedside.

"How are we feeling today Ms Meadows?" The nurse asked with a professional smile.

"Thirsty, very thirsty," she croaked.

"We can see to that," the nurse replied as she fetched a drink bottle from the bedside cabinet and placed the in-built straw to Laura's lips.

Laura sipped on the tepid water. The tap water was barely palatable but was refreshing, nonetheless. "What time is it? What day?" she asked.

The nurse looked at her watch. "It's just past noon on the 5th of November… Friday. You were brought in yesterday evening in a state of exhaustion and shock. You had a few cuts and bruises and a very nasty bump to the head, but we have cleaned you up, and the painkillers will help you over the worst of your injuries. If you need anything else, just call." With that, the nurse fluffed Laura's pillow, added a note to her chart and left the room.

In the safety of the hospital, Laura looked up at the ceiling and tried to recount the past day's events. She couldn't make sense of any of it.

Her thoughts were interrupted by a knock at the door. A different nurse came in and gently plopped a lunch tray onto her bed. The woman left without a word or even a hint that Laura existed. Laura shifted to a sitting position and looked at the 'food' on the tray. It appeared less than appetising. She picked up a fork and prodded at some gelatinous brown stuff on one of the plates. She put the fork down and pushed the tray away as far as she could without it falling onto the bed.

The throat-clearing noise grabbed her attention. Laura looked back at the door and smiled as she saw the large bouquet that Simmons was holding. He handed them over, and Laura took a long and deep breath of their delicious scent.

"How are you feeling, Laura?" Simmons asked, almost in a whisper.

"I'm fine, just a bit bruised. I hope to be home by this evening," she replied, adding, "They killed him, didn't they?"

He nodded. "They thought he had a bomb, Laura."

"He didn't want to harm me." she shook her head.

Simmons wasn't expecting her comment, "I want to hear everything, but I have an important meeting within the hour. We can talk about this later. If you can hang on until I get back, I can give you a lift home, and we can discuss what happened."

"That would be good," Laura replied.

Pointing at the tray, Simmons managed a wry smile and said, "Bon appetite!" and left for his meeting. Abrupt as usual, she thought, but kind, and he does have a sense of humour.

It was the first time he had ever been to the CIA headquarters, and Neil Simmons was taken aback by the ultra-secure meeting room in which he now sat. Around him were seated members of the higher echelons from some of the US's major government organisations – not to mention the imposing figure of the Vice President herself. Bob Dexter pressed the button to make the room safe – the light on the ceiling changed from red to green, and the transparent walls became frosted. Dexter welcomed Simmons to the Committee and recounted the events of the past couple of days to the group.

"The work of Laura Meadows at the GSFC has added more credibility to the works of Richard Fairbrother. As you can see in the image on page three of your brief, there is a definite and sizeable non-natural structure on the Moon. At the moment, it's located just on the far side near the lunar north pole. However, because of the Moon's natural libration cycle, it should be in line-of-sight from Earth for a few days each month. As you can see by the shadows cast by the feature, it appears somewhat reminiscent of the ancient Stonehenge structure in England. However, I should add that the lunar structure is much larger. Now, from what we've interpreted from the Fairbrother papers, which, by the way, include some rudimentary sketches of Stonehenge, the discovery of the structure identifies something of a fixed reference point for some of the events predicted to follow. Specifically, and perhaps most alarmingly, is the prediction that the Chinese will get to the Moon within two years of us discovering the structure. From what we have gleaned, they already have, or will very soon discover, the structure themselves, and this spurs them to advance their lunar program by several years. As I see it, the main question is whether or not we can afford for the Chinese to get to the structure before us. Considering this is possibly the greatest discovery ever made, my immediate answer to this is an emphatic no!" Dexter scanned the room and saw nothing but nods of agreement. He noticed that Janet Cleo, the NSA chief, was unfolding a piece of paper she had taken out of her jacket pocket. Her eyes flicked between the briefing document and the note, and then she noisily cleared his throat. Simmons saw the cue, "Janet, do you have something to add?"

"You could say that," Cleo replied with a husky smoker's voice that matched her prematurely aged face, "Just before our meeting, I received a decrypted intercept from the Chinese Space Administration with the coordinates related to their lunar programme. If I'm not mistaken, they already know about the structure and plan to head there. All indications are that this location is the target of their next lunar probe and their preferred landing site."

Simmons motioned Jones for the piece of paper, looked at it and flicked through his report until he found the page he was after. He nodded, "Yep, they are using a different datum, but these coordinates look to be within a stone's throw of the structure."

Bob Dexter took over, mumbled an obscenity under his breath that even the worst lip reader could understand and continued, "OK, it looks as if we have an imperative. We know that the Chinese know, but they probably don't know that we do. This makes all the more urgent the bigger question: how in Hell do we get to the Moon before the Chinese?"

The room was silent, but Bob could imagine the whirring of the cogs in each of their heads. He knew that this problem was well outside the fields of expertise of most of those in the room. "Does anyone have any suggestions?" he asked.

Simmons still felt uncomfortable surrounded by such power brokers but flicked a finger in the air. "I think I have a solution that may be feasible both in terms of budget and time constraints."

"You have the floor, Neil." Bob motioned Simmons to stand as he sat down.

Simmons cleared his throat. "A few years ago, when President Obama cancelled the 'Return to the Moon' program and scaled back the now cancelled Constellation program, a few of us had a lunchtime discussion about how we could get to the Moon and back safely using predominantly existing technology. One of my senior analysts, Dr Brad Sommers, provided an elegant solution. It involves two launches; one uses the Delta IV Heavy to send a fuel tank into low Earth orbit. We then send up a modified shuttle assembly with a small lander and extra fuel in its bay to rendezvous with the tank. Together this would provide the fuel necessary for trans-lunar insertion. Theoretically, two launches and one spacewalk could get us there and back. The new space suits were designed and prototyped some time ago, and we could manufacture a set within weeks. The only things we need to create from scratch are the lunar lander module and fuel tank. Then we need to work out the shuttle modifications to allow docking with the fuel tank and how to transfer propellants to the engines. Unlike the Apollo mission, a crew of seven can easily spend a month on the shuttle. The new generation space suits allow for excursions of two or three days at a time on the lunar surface. It may be uncomfortable, but it is within the design parameters. Furthermore, the lander could be configured to allow re-fuelling from the shuttle, enabling multiple trips to the surface."

Bob stood up and motioned Simmons to sit down. "How feasible is this proposal?" he asked.

Simmons replied, "Quite feasible. At that lunch, I was sceptical of Dr Sommers' approach and offered a decent bottle of Scotch if he could support his proposal. He went away and came back the next day with five pages of maths and calculations that showed it was indeed doable."

Bob turned to the head of the table, "Madam Vice President, I believe that time is imperative, and we appear to have a viable solution, as tenuous as that may be. If you agree, the President needs to be informed to obtain congressional funding for this project, which must remain at the highest level of secrecy."

The Vice President replied, "I agree with you, Bob, and I will brief the President as soon as I get back to the Whitehouse. The shuttle fleet is to be retired soon, but one of the museums may just have to wait for their exhibit. Dr Simmons, you must get a team together to make this plan a reality. I see from the brief that Dr Sommers already knows about the lunar feature. If this is so and he has the appropriate expertise to help, I would like him to be a part of the team, along with Dr Laura Meadows, who made the discovery. I will arrange for the necessary security clearances as soon as I get back to my office. I would also appreciate it if you could provide me with a summary of your plan ASAP, in lay terms, for us non-scientists."

Bob Dexter retook the floor. "If there is nothing else, then we can adjourn this meeting. I'll ensure that you all get a copy of Dr Simmons' report and a summary of this meeting."

It was nearly four o'clock in the afternoon, and Laura just stared out of the window, looking at the red and gold hues of the leaves on the maple trees that lined the section of highway they were on. She had the window open enough for the cold autumn breeze to hit her face. The car's heater was on with the vent pointed directly at her head with the fan up high. She found the change of sensation from hot to cold and back again somewhat comforting and refreshing. She reluctantly brought her hand to the back of her head and felt the large bump she had received the day before. It had begun to sting again – the painkillers were starting to wear off.

"How are you feeling, Laura?" Simmons asked.

"I'm OK. I'm just trying to work out what happened. This guy had been watching me for some time. The crackpot told me he was destined to prepare me to fly to the heavens to meet God. I thought he was going to kill me."

Simmons thought about what she said, "Well, you're safe now, Laura. I'm just thankful that a bump on the head is the worst of your injuries. You'll be home within the hour, so take plenty of rest over the weekend and take as much time off as you need. However, I need to talk to you and Brad regarding your report on the lunar structure – as soon as you are up to it. I'll get Tina to schedule a time for this if it's OK with you."

In response, Laura simply nodded and continued gazing vacantly out the window. The events of the past day had felt like an eternity. Exhausted by her ordeal, every time she closed her eyes, all she could envision were the piercing blue eyes of her kidnapper staring back at her – haunting her, along with the tune he kept humming. She wished that she could forget them.

# Chapter Seventeen

The anger in his eyes was palpable as he scanned the text on the page he held. With a stiff jaw and clenched teeth, the veins on his forehead rose to prominence. Ran threw the pages onto his desk, lent with both knuckles on the table and vented his anger towards the person who sat uncomfortably on the other side. "How did they get this information? Do we have a spy in our midst? A traitor?"

The young man who was the target of Ran's wrath gulped before he could reply, his head low and eyes staring at the floor, "We... we don't think so, Sir. It appears that they have intercepted and decrypted our communications. I will arrange for our security protocols to be changed and tightened at once."

Regaining some composure, Ran responded in a more even tone, "No, don't change a thing. I want complete control of what information we send out over that channel. I want you to get in touch with our US asset to find out what the Americans know and their plans. You can go."

"Yes, Sir." the young man said as he stood up with his head kept low and eyes averted as he literally backed out of Ran's office.

Ran pondered the behaviour of the young security analyst he had just berated. Such 'old school' behaviour without the balls to look him in the eye – how traditional, he thought – how pathetic. However, he was a bright analyst and had identified their information leak to the Americans. His thoughts then wandered to the situation at hand. It was unfortunate that the Americans had discovered the target of their next probe – an unmanned rover, but did they know about the feature? Probably not. But could he take the chance? Would the information they have make them look closer at the target area? Possibly. He rubbed at his chin and tried to put himself in the position of the Americans. What would they do if they wanted a closer look? Given the disarray of their space programme, it would take a year or two to prepare and launch a dedicated probe. They were more likely to re-task the Lunar Reconnaissance Orbiter to get a closer look. That's what he would do. He smiled at that thought. His team had cracked the encryption of the LRO's data feeds not long after it was inserted into lunar orbit. Although they were unable to control the probe's path, they were able to retrieve sent imagery as quickly as the Americans. Ran sat at his computer and typed a brief email to the person in charge of monitoring the probes of other countries, ordering him to pay special attention to the LRO and to inform him of any orbital changes. He also requested that all data sent from the probe be captured and archived for future analysis.

Ran turned his attention back to the Americans. There's no way they could get men back onto the lunar surface within a decade – they didn't have the money, facilities or willpower to do so. However, they had proven themselves experts at robotic missions, and if pushed, they could potentially get a sophisticated remote-controlled rover to the Moon within a year or so. Ran gave a large sigh as he realised he needed to talk to his superiors as a shake-up and further clandestine advancement of their lunar programme may be required.

# Chapter Eighteen

Laura sat at her station and flicked through the report she had prepared before her abduction. She found it difficult to concentrate and realised that although she had been staring at the page, she hadn't read anything. Perhaps she should have taken a few extra days off work. Then again, her tiny apartment afforded even fewer distractions to take her mind off her recent ordeal. She looked at her watch. Over 40 minutes had passed, and she hadn't managed to do a scrap of productive work. She turned around to see Brad standing at the entrance to her cubicle. "How long have you been standing there, Brad?" she asked.

"Not long," he replied. He had been there for a few minutes watching Laura and noticing the scratches on her face, hands and arms that she had attempted to hide with makeup. "Simmons noticed you were in and wanted to meet with both of us ASAP." With a look of genuine concern, he added, "Are you OK, Laura?"

"I'm fine, Brad," Laura replied. "I'm just a bit bewildered over what happened. I'm hoping the FBI will fill me in on the guy's motives... if there are any." With Brad, she picked up her report and headed off to Simmons' office in silence.

Simmons sat at his desk, thumbing through Laura's report, when Tina opened the door for Brad and Laura. He looked up, waved them both in and motioned them to take a seat. A small nod and a slight smile were all that Simmons managed towards Laura. Although a minor gesture, Laura took this to mean 'welcome back'. He got straight down to business. "Laura, and Brad, you are both being re-tasked to a project of utmost national importance. Brad, I've reassigned your current tasks, and Tina is giving those concerned the news. Both of you are getting a higher security clearance and will be reporting directly to me from now on. You are to discuss none of this with any other personnel, friends or family. Everything you are about to hear is classified Above Top Secret – do I make myself clear?"

Brad and Laura looked at each other, and in unison, they sat upright and nodded.

Simmons continued. "Good. If anyone asks, you are both working on a proposal for a new lunar laboratory for materials-based experiments. Let them know there's a snowball's chance of funding, but you have to go through the motions. Have I made myself clear?"

"Wow, Boss," Brad replied, "all of this is a bit out of left field. I assume that this has something to do with Laura's report?"

"Yes, it does. But it also has as much to do with Laura's abduction." He looked at her to gauge her response – she was visibly taken aback.

"My abduction is related to my report?" Laura asked with a gasp.

Simmons nodded and explained events to date, including Leo Helfgott, Richard and Peter Fairbrother, the papers, and project Star Gate. As Simmons gave his monologue, he noticed, with some amusement, the expressions of both Laura and Brad – confusion, disbelief, bewilderment and some that he couldn't quite measure waved over their faces. He wrapped up, "This is a multi-agency effort, and your initial duty will be re-tasking the LRO to get the best look at the structure that Laura discovered. Based on the findings of that exercise, we may be looking at a manned mission."

Brad shook his head in disbelief, "Am I on Candid Camera, Boss? I'm having trouble taking this all in."

"No, I'm not pulling your pisser," Simmons responded in uncharacteristically blunt language. "I was just as confused and suspicious as you when I was brought up to speed. One thing I haven't mentioned is that we may have a tight schedule. By all indications, the Chinese are aware of the structure, and their next lunar probe will land there. I don't have to tell you that we want to keep the upper hand, hence the secrecy and the need to reassign both of you. By the way, the project has a name: "Project Moonshadow."

Laura made a loud huffing noise that drew the attention of both men. She shook her head in another display of disbelief.

"What is it?" Neil asked.

"You're going to think this is crazy, Boss, but the guy who abducted me... Peter Fairbrother, you say... he kept humming a tune most of the time. It was so annoying. I couldn't put my finger on what tune it was, but it has just clicked. It was Cat Steven's Moonshadow!"

"Nothing about this surprises me at the moment. However, let's get to work. Brad, do the calculations to re-task the LRO to get shots of the structure from as many viewpoints and illumination angles as possible. Try not to burn too much propellant, as we would like to continue with the planned mission once we've got our shots. Laura, work with Brad on the LRO for now. Later today, we will be meeting with Leo Helfgott. As we speak, copies of all the notes and tapes Peter Fairbrother had in his van and at the warehouse are on their way here. Given your recent ordeal, I need you to go through these and see if you can make any sense of it. Now, hand over your key cards." Neil motioned for these and handed them each a new one, complete with details of their revised security status. "These will give you access to general-purpose room two, which is your base of operations. It's a large and essentially unused room that should draw little attention from your colleagues. We've installed computer stations and secure communications with the other agencies concerned. Try to keep a low profile and do some non-sensitive work in your cubicles to prevent raising people's suspicions."

It was clear that the meeting was over in Simmons' classic style. Brad and Laura got out of their chairs, left the office and headed directly for their new mission operations room. Neither spoke on their short walk... both were trying to digest the information they had just been made privy to.

Brad was the first to talk outside the mission's operation room, "Would you like to do the honours, Ms Meadows?" He waved his shiny new key card in front of her.

Laura smiled and placed her key card on the sensing pad. The door latch clicked, and she pushed her way through the door. Brad was right behind her and couldn't help but gasp when he saw the hardware in the room. Large plasma displays adorned every wall, including a massive

100-inch screen on the far wall. Underneath that was a credenza full of stationary, toners and inks. Beside that was a brand-new large format colour inkjet printer. A conference table/layout table occupied the centre of the room, and there were six workstations, each with brand new computers sporting four top-of-the-range large flat-panel displays. In one corner was a small kitchenette with a well-stocked refrigerator and coffee machine.

"Can you believe all of this, Laura?" Brad asked with a whistle.

She shook her head, "It looks as if they are planning for more than just the two of us in here... just look at all this gear!"

Brad sat at the conference table and opened the large white lever-arch file. There was a notepad and pencil and on the top page was a message 'Close your jaw Brad and get to work! Simmons.' He smiled at the comment and moved the notepad to reveal the LRO command and control guide. He slid the pad over to Laura, "He has spoken!" he said and commenced to flick through the manual, looking for the information needed to re-task the Lunar Reconnaissance Orbiter.

It was nearly noon as Tina escorted Leo into Simmons' office and promptly left, only to return a few minutes later with a pot of freshly brewed coffee and a plate of sandwiches.

"So, Leo, what have you discovered from Peter Fairbrother's effects?" Simmons asked as he helped himself to a sandwich.

"There's a lot to go through, Neil. He seemed to work a lot differently from his father. Whereas Richard Fairbrother created pages upon pages of scribbles and pictographs – through visions as it were, Peter seemed to have more of an 'audio' access to possible future events. There are literally dozens of audio cassettes and, more recently, videotapes of Peter talking, often rambling, about things that don't appear to make much sense to us at the moment. Bob Dexter is in the process of getting everything transcribed and put into a searchable database for us. A team of people are working on it, so we should have something within the next day or two. Apart from audio and video tapes, Peter did leave behind a couple of notebooks, most of which focus on the comings and goings of Laura Meadows. When the agents shot him, he was holding a small black pocketbook. On the first page was written 'Imperative Laura gets this'. I haven't had an opportunity to see the rest of the pocketbook's contents, but I'll have a copy delivered here as soon as possible."

Neil digested Leo's update as he worked his way through his lunch. "I guess your main task will be going through everything we have from Richard and Peter, looking for commonalities, correct?"

Leo nodded.

Neil continued. "Well, as you are aware, both Laura Meadows and Brad Sommers have been indoctrinated into this project, and a base of operations has been set up just down the corridor. For whatever reason, it appears that Laura is somehow central to present and future events. If it suits you, I would like you to work here with us and involve Laura with your analysis as much as possible. We have plenty of computing power and full secure video conferencing facilities to keep in touch with other Project Moonshadow members and plenty of room to spread out. Brad and Laura only moved in there a couple of hours ago. They are currently working on the calculations to re-task the Lunar Reconnaissance Orbiter to get ultra-high-resolution imagery of the structure."

"Not to mention trying to get their heads around all of this." Leo chuckled and continued, "But having a base of operations here makes complete sense, so yes, I would be more than happy to work out of your offices here."

Neil gave a nod of appreciation and passed Leo a lanyard, complete with a set of security credentials and a swipe card. "No need to go through the visitor process from now on, Leo. I've arranged a car bay close to the entrance, and Tina is currently sourcing some accommodation for you nearby. This key card should give you access to everything you need. If not, just let me know, and I'll sort things out. Now, if you're up for a little walk, we can go to the operations room, and I'll introduce you to Laura and Brad.

Laura and Brad sat at the same computer terminal. Brad pointed at various features on the screen and was bringing Laura up to speed on the Lunar Reconnaissance Orbiter's control suite. Both were so transfixed in what they were doing that neither noticed Leo nor Neil enter the room.

With a guttural clearing of his throat, Simmons caught their attention and made the customary introductions. Laura instantly took a liking to the old man, who, apart from skin colour, greatly reminded her of her grandfather – a dear person who passed away when Laura was just seven but who, in that short time, had inspired her to pursue science and her dreams.

They all took a seat at the large meeting table. Neil passed out several manila folders that contained copies of Richard Fairbrother's notes and minutes from previous meetings of the Moonshadow Project Committee. Brad couldn't help but give out a whistle when he saw the list of Committee members. It read like the Who's Who of the governmental aristocracy. Laura flicked through some of Fairbrother's notes, many of which had attached a page of Leo's interpretations.

Simmons began. "You three are the core brains of this operation, and I can recruit others as the need arises. I want Laura to work with Leo on the interpretation of the notes of Richard Fairbrother and the recordings of his son Peter. Are you OK with that – it won't be too distressing for you, will it?"

"I'm fine with it, Boss," she replied.

Simmons continued, "OK then, but if it gets too much for you, please let Leo or me know – we will understand. Laura, you will also be helping Brad with the re-tasking operations of the LRO and working out a viable way to retrofit a space shuttle to get us to the Moon and back." He looked at Brad, who had just recalled the bet they once had, "You can see why you are perfect for this task, Brad. Maybe there will be another bottle of Scotch in it for you. However, the requirements are a bit more complex than your original plan. We need a solution to get both a lander and a rover to the Moon's surface. According to Leo's interpretation, we need to get seven astronauts into lunar orbit and five people onto the surface with the ability to convey them potentially for several kilometres."

"That'll take more than a bottle of Scotch, Boss – a crate, maybe.

When we had our bet, we planned to get just two people onto the surface and back again. My calculations squeezed every piece of space out of the shuttle's cargo bay to do that. I can't see how we could fit a lander for five in the bay. As for a rover, there's the size and mass to consider, not to mention a way to get it out of the lander. It's a tall order, Boss." Brad replied.

"I don't expect it to be easy, Brad, but I'm sure you can come up with an 'outside-of-the-box' solution for us," Simmons replied with a hint of a grin. "How are you getting along with the LRO?" he asked.

Brad responded. "I've done most of the calculations, Boss. In the next day or two, we should be able to get several images of the structure from different altitudes and sun-angle directions. In fact, it may even be possible to get the LRO from its current 50km orbit to as low as 3km. That will give us a nominal resolution of around three centimetres. This will happen on the last few orbits so we can get an image of the entire structure at that resolution. From there, we should be able to get it back to its normal orbit. However, I estimate we will burn 30 to 40 percent of its remaining propellant supply. I will run some more simulations to see if that number can be reduced."

"The LRO mission has exceeded our expectations, so I don't see that fuel expenditure as much of an issue. Do what you need to do." Simmons said and then checked his watch. "Brad, are you expecting to uphold your honour today?"

Brad gave a confused look, followed by a wave of recognition. "With all that's been going on, I completely forgot, Boss. Are we OK to go?"

"I think we can spare half an hour for a bit of fun," Simmons replied. Looking at the puzzled expressions on the faces of Laura and Leo, he explained the long-running tradition at the GSFC – the annual paper aeroplane competition. One day every year, workers at the GSFC had the chance to show off their engineering skills by constructing a paper aircraft launched from the roof of the seven-story administration building. Trophies are awarded for the longest time aloft, the furthest distance travelled, and the highest altitude. The rules were simple. The aircraft must be made exclusively from paper, and glue sticks are the only adhesive allowed. Brad prided himself on winning the time and distance records for the past three years. This year he was hoping to win all three.

Brad ran to his cubicle to grab his entry, and all four made their way to the elevator. Fortunately for Leo, the elevator on the administration building went all the way to the roof. At the top were about twenty or so participants and a similar number of observers. As it happened, Brad was just in time to launch his entry. He quickly reviewed the whiteboard that contained the standings of the other participants – the weather conditions were such that records were unlikely to be broken this year. Licking a finger and raising it to the air, Brad gauged the wind direction and oriented himself appropriately. With a flair for the dramatic and with a fluid motion of his shoulder, arm and wrist, he launched his small delta-winged glider and watched with satisfaction as it sailed off the top of the building. The paper plane hit a light thermal rose a little, then dipped and bobbed away from the building. The seconds felt like minutes as they passed. Looking at his watch, he realised he had just won the time aloft prize again. He turned to Neil to see his reaction, but he was engaged in a conversation with Leo. When the plane finally landed, Brad raised a fist as he realised he had also won the distance challenge. Unfortunately, the altitude prize eluded him once again.

Brad walked to collect his trophies from the camp table that the competition organisers had set up, but Neil was there to intervene.

"Not just yet, Brad. We have a late entry." Simmons said as he pointed towards Leo. "Do you have any objections?"

Brad looked towards Leo – he didn't even have a piece of paper in his hand. Intrigued, he grew a large grin, bowed his head, and returned to the launching area. Everyone watched with curiosity as Leo reached into his top pocket and extracted a paper handkerchief. With trembling fingers, he carefully separated the two plys, and with one of the layers in his frail hand, he dropped it over the edge. Instantly wind rotor up the side of the building caught the tissue paper, and it wafted skyward and back over the building. It then entered the exhaust stream of the air conditioning unit and gained additional altitude. Caught in a light breeze, the paper tissue entered a strong thermal. It tossed, turned and tumbled into the distance until it was entirely out of sight.

Brad's jaw dropped as he realised that Leo, a non-engineer, had conceived and implemented a solution in a matter of seconds that had just won him all three records. All the spectators on the roof clapped and cheered at Leo's victory. On the other hand, all the entrants looked shocked and not a bit embarrassed. Eventually, they all joined in with the clapping and cheering. Leo, in turn, gave a slight bow and extended a nod to Brad.

Brad spoke with Simmons. "He's one amazing old-timer."

"He told me he wanted to test his lateral thinking and improvisation skills. I think he passed with flying colours! Not to mention it's good to see the engineers get knocked down a peg or two – you included." Simmons responded with a grin. "Perhaps you can take a leaf out of his book regarding the lunar lander and rover problem."

With a broad and genuine smile, Brad nodded and went over to congratulate Leo on his achievement.

# Chapter Nineteen

Brad sat at the meeting desk and busily scribbled on a large sheet of paper. After several hours, a solution to the problem of fitting a lander and rover for five people into the space shuttle cargo bay still eluded him. It was simply not possible. He tore the sheet off the large pad, crumpled it up and tossed it into a nearby bin, almost full of similarly scrunched-up pages. He mumbled under his breath until a loud ping from a computer caught Brad's attention. The simulation of his changes to the LRO's orbit was complete. He made his way over to the terminal. He smiled when he saw that the calculations were accurate and that his parameters would allow for several images of the structure from different Sun angles and altitudes. At least something was working in his favour. He picked up the phone and placed a call to Simmons to give him the news. After a few seconds of conversation, Simmons gave Brad the go-ahead to retask the LRO. A few minutes at his computer terminal allowed Brad to transfer the parameters from the simulator to the LRO command suite. His palms were sweating, and his hands were shaking a little as he checked, double-checked and triple-checked the command set he had just uploaded. The LRO cost almost $600 million to build and place into a lunar orbit. A slight mistake now could lead to a catastrophic loss of the orbiter.

Finally sure that he had entered everything correctly, he clicked on the 'Commit' icon and entered his username and password into the window that appeared. After entering these, Brad was presented with a final screen: 'Click OK to commit or Cancel to abort.' With a deep breath, he clicked on the OK icon. The main window displayed a list of times the LRO would re-orient and fire its thrusters to adjust its orbit to capture the required images. At the bottom-left of the screen was a picture of the Moon. A red line showed the current path of the probe, and next to it was a list of numbers that showed the LRO's orbital parameters, including altitude, velocity and the current lunar latitude and longitude. He turned to Laura to boast about his calculations and control of a multi-million-dollar probe, but she was talking with Leo about the Fairbrother papers. Looking at the documents on the desk, Brad felt quite uncomfortable about the whole situation. He returned to the meeting desk and continued scribbling possible lander/rover solutions on his pad.

Laura rolled her hair around the index finger of her left hand as she looked over each page to see what she could glean from the Fairbrother notes. Playing with her hair while she was in deep thought was something she had done since childhood. Some of her schoolmates teased her about it, but even 20 years later, she couldn't break the habit.

Leo passed page twelve of Richard Fairbrother's notes to Laura. "This is probably one of the most important pieces of paper that fixed the timeline. I'm not sure if you know this, but I discovered these notes in 2004. I found references to events that occurred years after these notes were written, including 9/11 and the Challenger and Columbia disasters."

Laura looked at the page. There were scribbles of the Sun, Earth, Moon and stars. Two curved lines, complete with arrowheads, led from the Earth to the Moon, one from the US and another from China. From the Moon was a thick line curving around the Sun to the stars with the words 'OUR DESTINY AWAITS' in large capital letters at the other end. Richard Fairbrother had overwritten the text several times for added emphasis. At the bottom of the page was a crude drawing of a satellite. This one was rectangular with two stubby solar panels and a boom with a small parabolic antenna at the end. Next to the sketch were the letters 'LRO'.

Laura looked at the date in the corner of the page – 3/1/1996 – and smiled at the drawing of the satellite. "That's not a bad artist's impression of the LRO, considering Richard Fairbrother drew it years before the project was even conceived."

Leo nodded. "Yes, I realised it was a satellite at once and that the letters LRO were likely to be an acronym. You couldn't believe my surprise when I discovered shortly after finding these papers that the GSFC was planning to build and launch this very same probe. This discovery led to the next page of importance." He handed Laura another page.

This page was considerably more abstract. There was a drawing of what looked like a funeral wreath and a simple landscape complete with scribbles of grass, sheep and cows. On the side of the page was written in Fairbrother's hand 'GSFC / SHE IS THE KEY TO OUR DESTINY!!!'. At the top of the page was the same date – 3/1/1996.

"I don't get it?" Laura said. "What do a wreath and a landscape have to do with anything?"

"I didn't get it at first. Actually, I didn't get it correct at all, come to think of it. This page is why we didn't get Simmons involved until recently. This pictogram represents a name, Laura – your name!"

Laura looked back at the page but was confused. "How do you get my name from this?"

Leo smiled. "Well, I didn't exactly. The wreath you refer to is a laurel, and the landscape is a field – or a meadow, to be exact. I initially went through the employee list of the GSFC but couldn't find any match. From then on, I received regular updates about new staff appointments, and you can imagine my surprise when the name Laura Meadows appeared. I must admit I was expecting a Laurel Fields."

With the excitement of retasking the LRO subsiding and the impasse he faced with finding a lander and rover design, Brad stopped scribbling and listened in on the conversation. He re-seated himself next to Laura and looked over the two pages. "Spooky but disturbing," he said.

"Why disturbing?" Leo responded.

"Well, it appears that this Fairbrother guy is a modern-day Nostradamus. He has seen the future. Does that mean that our future is fixed? If so, does that imply that everything is pre-destined to unfold in a certain way? It quashes the concept of free will and fate, and I find that very disturbing."

Leo responded. "I have wrestled with similar thoughts since I first got involved with this project. It's one of the reasons that we've essentially been observers, as we're unsure what would happen should we attempt to interfere with events too much. Most of Fairbrother's notes make sense only after the events to which they relate have already happened, and I guess that doesn't allow us to tinker with what he has prognosticated. However, I agree with you that the revelations by Richard Fairbrother preclude the possibility that the future is somehow fixed and that we are just characters in some play in which we actors have no control. Although we may believe that we have free will, we unknowingly work to a script. I, too, find that very disturbing. I expect that as this project progresses, we'll get some theoretical physicists, theologians and philosophers to battle it out and provide possible explanations and consequences. However, for now, we must accept that there is something of significance in Fairbrother's papers. Competing with the Chinese adds some measure of urgency to understanding what's going on."

Brad nodded in agreement. Tired of thinking about a lander/rover solution for the shuttle, he diverted his attention to the Fairbrother papers and provided Leo with interpretations of parts he thought significant. It appeared that Leo had made some sense of only a few percent of Fairbrother's material.

"I recognise that!" Brad exclaimed as he pointed at one of the doodles on the page. It's a map of the London underground. I bet those stars represent the locations of the terror bombings in 2005. I did a macabre tour of London last year, visiting the sites of the Ripper murders and where the bombs went off." He pointed at parts of the sketch, "That's the circle line where two bombs went off, and that's the Piccadilly line where the third explosion occurred."

Leo took notes from Brad's explanation. Up until a few minutes ago, Leo sensed that Brad was very sceptical about the Fairbrother papers. However, Brad's identification of a link between one innocuous sketch and an actual event caused all his scepticism to evaporate. Brad was rapidly becoming hooked as firmly as Leo.

Leo cleared his throat gutturally and handed Brad and Laura a single page each. "This page is the last page of Richard Fairbrother's notes. This page doesn't take much interpretation, and it scares the living crap out of me; excuse my language. This single page is the reason why Project Moonshadow even exists."

Leo remained silent as he let Brad and Laura analyse the page. A circle and some shading depicted the Earth, in the traditional form, with the Americas to the left and Europe and Asia on the right. Passing between the two continents were many incomplete arcs, representing the parabolic trajectories of intercontinental ballistic missiles. Richard Fairbrother had predicted all-out nuclear war and the razing of humanity.

It was quarter past ten at night, and Leo had long since gone home. Laura was at the meeting table looking at the Fairbrother notes while eating noodles from a carton. Brad was at his computer watching the status of the LRO.

"Laura, we're going to get our first look at ALF-1 from a 20km altitude. Do you want to see this?" Brad asked.

Laura leapt to her feet and jogged to Brad's side with no need for a second invitation.

Usually, the feed from the LRO gets spooled to hard drives before being processed into individual image frames. However, Brad had configured a dedicated buffer that allowed him to see the ALF-1 structure the moment they received the data. On a second monitor, an image rapidly appeared line by line. The ALF-1 feature was in the centre of the image, with each pixel representing an area of about 25cm x 25cm. Laura and Brad gave out a collective gasp as they saw the structure.

"It's huge!" Laura said with amazement. "It looks like it was engineered directly from the Lunar surface. What do you think?"

Brad began to alter the brightness and contrast of the image to enhance various aspects of the structure. "It looks like a building complex of some sort, and at this level of detail, it looks well constructed. But I cannot make out any windows or doors, so I don't think it's a building per se. It still looks a hell of a lot like Stonehenge, though."

"What's that in the centre?" Laura asked.

Brad shook his head and used his mouse to zoom into the feature. He adjusted the gamma of the image to maximise the local contrast.

"Is it just me, or does that look like a ramp going into the subsurface?" Brad remarked.

"That's exactly what it looks like. Can we get a printout of this and the whole structure on the large format printer?"

Brad was one step ahead of her. Even before she had finished her request, Brad had sent the image to the printer, which they heard initialising in the background, followed by the gentle swish and swoosh of the print head as it moved back and forth along the entire width of the 36-inch-wide paper roll.

Shortly after it had been seen by Laura and Brad, Ran stared at the detailed image of the lunar structure. The data analyst had informed him earlier in the day that the Lunar Reconnaissance Orbiter had changed its path and was due to pass over the feature at a lower-than-normal altitude. Within an hour of being taken, Ran held a copy of the 20km altitude imagery in his hand. It's fantastic, he thought. This raises many implications – the first being the realisation of absolute proof of intelligent life beyond Earth. Who knows what secrets and technologies this structure may contain? The Americans, no doubt, will find a way of returning to the Moon now, but they must not be the first. In a new word processing document, Ran began to draft a brief about his discovery and the imperative to get his astronauts to the Moon to investigate the structure. He intended to send the note directly to the Politburo Standing Committee of the Communist Party with a request to discuss the matter with Hu Jintao himself, the Paramount Leader of the country, and a person who would be just as shocked as he should the Americans get there first. "We must be as cunning as a monkey," he muttered as he outlined his plan in the document to give them the upper hand.

# Chapter Twenty

Most of the Committee members had hastily cancelled their previous engagements to make time for the unscheduled gathering. As usual, Bob Dexter opened the meeting.

"Gentlemen and Ladies, we have just received high-resolution imagery from the Lunar Reconnaissance Orbiter of the structure we have designated ALF-1. As you can see in your briefing document, the LRO captured this image from an altitude of 20km with a nominal pixel resolution of 25cm. The structure is large – approximately 800 metres across and is not a natural feature. The resolution is such that we can appreciate the precision of the structure's construction. Although the LRO does not contain a spectrograph, evaluation of the probes LAMP and LEND instrument supports the conclusion that it was carved out of the lunar regolith rather than placed or built there. Early tomorrow, the LRO will pass over the central portion of the structure at an altitude of just three kilometres. This will allow us to obtain imagery with a nominal resolution of two to three centimetres. The ramp at the direct centre of the structure that appears to lead into the lunar subsurface will be of the most interest in this image. God only knows what we are going to find down there."

The Committee members flicked through the notes – most shook their heads in disbelief as the farcical project became a real one.

"Thanks for the update, Bob." The mellow voice of the President resonated around the room. "The Vice President has kept me abreast with your previous meetings, and I agree that we need to get Americans back to the Moon as a matter of the greatest urgency. We know that the Chinese are aware of the structure, and although they are several years away from launching a manned mission, we are years further behind them – even if we re-boot the Constellation programme today."

Looking directly at Simmons, the President continued. "As you outlined in a previous meeting, getting a shuttle into lunar orbit may be the only viable way we could get to the Moon quickly and beat the Chinese there. What will it cost to get us back to the Moon within, say, two years?"

Everyone looked towards Simmons for an answer. With a few scribbles on his notepad, he replied, "A shuttle launch costs on average $450 million and a Delta IV heavy costs around $170 million, and we may need two of these. Another $20 to $30 million for the space suits. The current unknown costs are for the fit out of the shuttle bay, the price of an external fuel tank and the lander and rover solution. I imagine we won't get much change out of two or maybe even three billion dollars."

The President smiled at the estimate with relief in his eyes. It was a lot less than he had expected. "If you can do it for that, I would indeed be a very happy man. NASA currently gets around $18 billion a year. I should be able to find the extra funds without going on bended knee to Congress. We all know how much they like me at the moment, given the global financial crisis and the measures I've implemented to jump-start the economy." He finished with the chuckle for which he was famous.

With a nod of acknowledgement, Bob Dexter took the floor. "Thank you, Mr President." Then, addressing the committee, "One thing we need to look at is a good cover story. It's going to make news that a shuttle is being kept back for a future launch and the Chinese, not to mention the Russians, are sure to get suspicious."

The Committee members chatted amongst themselves for the remainder of the meeting, coming up with several different options, some simple, others complex, and more than a few that were completely absurd.

The effect such a fantastic discovery can have on one's drive and vitality was amazing. Leo had the focus of a university graduate as he continued to work through Fairbrother's notes. Laura and Brad were getting by on only a few hours of rest a night. Like children on Christmas Eve, they were too excited to sleep. However, their ultimate Christmas present still lay out of reach, around a quarter of a million miles away – so close yet so far.

Brad sat at the layout table with Leo and scoured through the Fairbrother notes whilst sipping on strong coffees. Brad's main priority of finding a lander and rover solution to fit into the shuttle bay had eluded him. He had hit a brick wall and felt he was getting nowhere. It was possible to squeeze a lander into the shuttle bay, but there was simply no way to accommodate a rover. The only alternative he could see was to send two shuttles – but from the outset, Simmons had told him that this was not an option as it would draw too much attention – both from the American public, the Chinese and the Russians, no doubt.

Brad switched his attention back to the notes in front of him. In one corner was a small drawing of a few stick figures sitting on circles. He turned to the next page and saw a similar illustration. Several pages had similar sketches in the corner. Brad smiled – he hadn't seen one of these for years – it was a miniature flick-book. Brad had gone through a phase from primary school to university, where he adorned the corners of his notebooks with short animations. His favourite flick animation was of his seventh-grade English teacher's head swelling and exploding. He created it when he was 12 and still had the notebook at home. Brad tapped the edges of the pages on the table so they all lined up, then flicked the corners to reveal the animation. Brad watched the animation a few times, but the paper was a bit thin to flick through. The stick figures bounced up and down on the circles – they were sitting on space hoppers, an inflated toy popular with children in the early 1970s. He smiled at the nostalgia of the animation, and as he took another sip of his coffee when the cogs within his head began to turn, and he stared into the distance. His eyes slowly widened, and a smile started across his lips. "That's it!" he muttered. Leaning back and pointing his face to the ceiling, he exclaimed much louder, "That's IT!" and chuckled.

Brad's outburst grabbed the attention of both Leo and Laura. Leo was the first to comment. "It sounds to me that you have had a Eureka moment. Am I right?"

"You could say that, Leo. Fairbrother has solved my problem of squeezing a lander and a rover into the shuttle bay with room to spare!

Leo, this is a 'paper tissue' moment." Brad replied, referring to Leo's triumph at the recent paper aircraft competition.

"Are you going to enlighten us then?" Laura asked from her workstation.

After composing his thoughts, Brad moved to the large whiteboard and took the cap off a marker. The sweet, almost addictive smell of xylene from the pen tantalised his nostrils. "Well, the solution is quite simple. We don't have room for a lander and a rover, so we must dispense with one. But as we need both, we are left with only one solution – a device which is a lander and a rover. Fairbrother's animation provided the answer – we build a 'moonhopper'. Instead of just providing a lander with lunar descent and ascent capabilities, we design it to make short jumps or hops from place to place whilst on the surface. This will require more fuel than a conventional lander, so we need to accommodate this. First, we can use carbon fibre to keep the mass down and to allow a faster landing speed. Second, we add a larger fuel tank. However, we must sacrifice something else to accommodate the larger fuel payload. Can you guess what that is?" Brad asked with a smile.

Leo and Laura glanced at each other and shrugged their shoulders in almost perfect union.

Brad continued, "It's quite simple, guys; we dispense with the actual habitation module. Pure genius if I don't say so myself."

Puzzled, Laura was the first to ask the obvious question. "How do the astronauts survive the trip from the shuttle to the surface and back without a habitation module?"

"That's the best bit, Laura. NASA has already designed, built and tested the next-generation spacesuit for the cancelled Constellation programme. These are quite unlike anything created before; an astronaut can wear one for several days before it requires maintenance. Our brief is for an eight-to-twelve-hour excursion to the surface, and the new suits easily allow for that. The moonhopper that I propose will look nothing like its Apollo counterpart. Instead, it will be a basic frame to which we strap the astronauts. The frame comprises a fuel tank, storage compartment, rocket motor and retro packs. It will be the ultimate amusement park ride if you like. This proposal is attractive because NASA has already done much of the work. They are prototyping an upcoming Mars lander, and we can use that as a basis for our moonhopper. This lander's new reusable engines are lightweight, powerful, fuel-efficient, and reliable. It should be relatively easy to adapt these for our moonhopper."

"But what about redundancy systems in case of a problem with one of the suits?" Laura quizzed.

Brad mulled this one over for a few seconds before answering. "Laura, I'm not sure if you've seen the plans for the new suits. Unlike the old Apollo and shuttle ones, the Constellation spacesuits are a one-piece affair with a door on the back between the life support system and suit proper. They were designed to attach to the outside of a lunar habitation module. The astronaut climbs into the suit, secures the hatch and disengages from the module to get on their way. It is the first spacesuit that doesn't require any assistance to put on. I envisage an astronaut in trouble could dock with a central structure on the moonhopper and use this as a temporary refuge. It would be a squeeze, but doable nonetheless."

Leo nodded, "That seems to be an elegant solution, Brad. Let's hope that the math works out."

With a new-found sense of purpose, it was as if he was the only person in the room as Brad returned to his desk and began scribbling designs on paper and entering calculations onto his workstation computer.

# Chapter Twenty One

Laura leant against the railing of her stateroom balcony on the eighth deck of the Diamond Princess cruise ship. At almost 116,000 tonnes, the luxury cruise liner was currently on its way from Vancouver to Ketchikan, Alaska. The wind was calm, slightly on the cold side, but refreshing, nevertheless. She stared towards the horizon and recalled the moment a year ago to the day when Leo collapsed and died before her. She saw the life extinguish from his eyes and remembered the feeling of dread and of complete hopelessness that had engulfed her. There was nothing either of them could have done – his heart had given out. Laura had grown very fond of Leo, and she felt exceptionally sad on the first anniversary of his passing. As the anniversary approached, Laura had become increasingly agitated and uneasy. The recent death of Neil Armstrong, the first man to step on the Moon's surface, also of heart-related problems hit Laura hard. Armstrong was one of Laura's idols, and at the news of his passing, she made a spare-of-the-moment decision and booked herself on a seven-night Alaskan cruise. She just needed to get away and was relieved when Simmons authorised her leave without comment or question. She mulled over the past two years' events as she sipped on a glass of full-bodied Australian merlot. So much had happened. She had discovered an artificial structure on the surface of the Moon, she had been abducted, and had spent hours analysing every scrap of data she could gather about the alien Stonehenge, trying to figure out what it was. Was it a building, a base, a communications array, or simply a piece of artwork? As much as she tried, she couldn't get over Leo's insistence to the powers that be that she must be one of the five astronauts who would make the journey to the lunar surface to visit the structure first-hand. According to Richard Fairbrother's cryptic notes, Leo had made the case that she was pivotal to the whole mission.

The ramblings of Peter Fairbrother only strengthened that argument. Now, as she stood staring out at the water, she shivered at the thought that she would be actually going into space in less than a month. She will stand on the lunar regolith itself.

Laura took another sip of wine and stared at the sapphire blue sea. Thoughts came to her about the poor astronauts of the Chinese rocket disaster. It had been a little over 14 months since their rocket exploded after it had just cleared the launch tower. The three astronauts vaporised in an instant. It was the first of several launches to test and integrate systems for their eventual visit to the Moon. Rare for the Communist state, they had televised the launch live and kept rolling during the resulting disaster. Reminiscent of the Challenger disaster in 1986 and the effect it had on the American psyche, this terrible event plunged the whole of China into a state of shock. In the months following, the entire Chinese manned lunar programme had ground to a halt. The administrator of their space agency had disappeared – either fled or killed – and they released little new information about the future of their space programme. The disaster also had repercussions on the economy. After years of double-digit growth, China dipped into a momentary recession, which affected the economies of other countries around the world, with Australia and the USA the hardest hit.

Memories and emotions hit Laura's mind from all directions. She smiled as she recalled the day she had her photo taken, standing next to a model of the space shuttle. Dressed in a figure-hugging light blue jumpsuit and with one hand resting on the model, she remembered how happy she felt. Seeing the final press release photo with the Stars and Stripes in the background, she could hardly believe that she was looking at herself. She pulled out the mission patch from her trouser pocket, which she had carried with her since the day she received it. Showing a shuttle with a blazing trail orbiting a prominent 'Omega' character with 'II' as a subscript, the mission patch parodied the STS-135 badge that was supposed to represent the final (Omega) flight of the shuttle. Now, she was part of STS-Omega II, flying the shuttle Discovery to the Moon on a modified booster assembly. NASA had told the public that this mission was imperative if humanity wanted to return to the Moon and eventually go to Mars. There was no mention of the alien structure or the intention to land on the lunar surface. Instead, the publicity centre of NASA stressed how little was known about the effects of radiation beyond the reaches of Earth's protective magnetosphere. The Omega II mission was to be a long flight to test various new technologies to protect future manned missions from harmful radiation exposure. That was the cover story, and the public remained blissfully unaware.

Her drink finished, Laura went back into her stateroom and closed the sliding door behind her. The air conditioner hummed gently to bring the cabin's temperature up to something more comfortable. She placed her glass on the table and picked up the Princess Patter – a daily planner listing activities on the ship during the day. She checked the time on her watch and ran her finger down the list. Many things were going on throughout the day, but she did not feel like doing any of them. She felt she should treat the day as one of remembrance and reflection rather than indulgence. She decided that a lap or two of the promenade deck was what she needed. Laura checked her make-up and hair in the mirror. Although she was still young, she was acutely aware that she was showing the early signs of aging as she ran a brush through her hair. Everyone except for short-haired or bald people had 'wind hair' on a cruise ship, so Laura wasn't too fussed about making it look too neat – presentable would have to do. She was about to leave the stateroom when the phone on her bedside table rang.

She leaned over the bed with half a mind to ignore it and reached for the handset. She was surprised to hear the voice of Neil Simmons on the other end. He was even more abrupt than usual.

"Laura, do you have access to CNN or the Internet?" He asked.

"I think we get CNN," Laura replied as she fumbled for the remote control. From the manner and the tone of his voice, Laura instantly knew that something significant was up.

"Switch it on if you can. I can't talk much about this as this line is insecure, but it appears that our friends in the east have not been completely honest with us. We'll have to bring our schedule forward, and we are looking at a window in the next couple of days."

"What's going on?" she tuned into CNN and saw an amateur

video of a rocket launch. The scrolling text at the bottom of the screen indicated that the Chinese had, without warning, re-entered the manned-space age.

"We need you back here ASAP for prep. Where is your next port of call?"

"The cruise just started yesterday. We are at sea all day today, and we don't get into Ketchikan until tomorrow."

Simmons was quiet at the other end, and the few seconds of silence felt much longer. "I'm afraid we need you back sooner than that. I'll arrange for a helicopter to come and pick you up."

Laura gulped. "I've explored this ship Boss, and I'm pretty sure it doesn't have a helipad."

Simmons' voice sounded slightly lighter with his reply – he thought it was amusing. "Well, you're just going to have to put some of that astronaut training into practice. I'll be in touch." Without waiting for a response, the line went silent.

Laura placed the receiver back on its cradle, sat on the edge of the bed, and watched for a few more minutes as a CNN correspondent reviewed the little information about the unscheduled launch. She desperately wanted something to take her mind off the anniversary of Leo's passing, but she hadn't expected something so dramatic.

In his office at the CNSA, Ran sipped on a glass of vintage Krug as he watched the rocket clear the tower and rumble towards the heavens. It certainly is a good day, he thought to himself. His leadership had resulted in nothing short of a miracle in the months since the staged accident. The destruction of an expensive prototype was necessary to give the Americans a false sense of security, and it had worked a treat. As anticipated, the progress of the US shuttle mission noticeably slowed once the Americans believed the Chinese programme had stalled. The loss of three astronauts was regrettable but necessary, Ran assured himself. Now, eight years ahead of schedule, he was sending three brave men to the Moon. However, until the mission was shown to be a success, the public would be told little – only that the launch was a systems integration test. Only when the astronauts get to the Moon and return safely to Earth will the world be told they extended the mission to land on the Moon. Depending on what they discovered, the existence of the alien structure may be released or kept a national secret. But that was not for him to decide.

The champagne bubbles danced on his tongue, and he felt the blood rush to his head as he gloated at the glory of his achievement.

A few hours after the launch, the mood at Langley was the complete opposite. "How in Hell could this have happened without us knowing about it?" The President asked Bob Dexter.

Bob didn't like the new President. He didn't vote for him and often wondered why so many people did. "Quite frankly, Sir, they put one over on us and did it well. After China's rocket exploded, all our satellites showed that their space program had halted and that their main rocket assembly plant was more or less deserted. It looks as if the rocket just launched was constructed at the launch facility itself. They must have a good handle on the locations of our reconnaissance satellites because the images we have shown very little going on there. I'm sure they knew that we had cracked one of their communication channels and that they fed us misinformation to indicate that their program had stalled. It appears that Ran Kai Rong, the head of China's space program who went missing after the explosion, was spearheading the clandestine production of a new launch vehicle."

"This is less than acceptable. What do we do now?" The tone of the President's voice made everyone in the room feel uneasy. Everyone felt like a target, and all were wary of potential repercussions.

Simmons motioned his intention to talk. In an abrupt manner somewhat reminiscent of Hitler, the President made an approving gesture. Clearing his throat, Simmons began to speak. "As you may or may not know, Discovery is ready to go. Several technical issues have been fixed, and the only thing preventing an early launch is literally bureaucratic paperwork." We are notifying the astronauts, and it's possible to reach launch readiness within a day or two. Barring any major incident on the Chinese side, we are unlikely to get to the Moon before them. However, we will get there whilst they are still on the surface or shortly after they leave. If there are significant artefacts to be discovered, I doubt they will be able to record or take everything. I just hope they don't destroy what they can't take. I wouldn't put it past the bastards."

"I'm not sure how Chinese astronauts may approach being gate-crashed... are they likely to be armed?" Janet Cleo asked.

There were murmurings around the table at the prospect of taking weapons into space.

"Has anyone ever developed a sidearm for use in space?" General Carter of the USAF asked.

"I doubt the Chinese would have bothered taking any weapons with them. The environment is hostile enough, and they believe they have at least a month's head start on us. I don't think taking guns up there will be of any practical use." Simmons interjected.

Bob Dexter couldn't believe the raised subject matter and tried to bring the meeting to order. "Please, everyone, let's stick to the task at hand. First, is launching in the next few days practical or feasible?"

Bob saw Simmons nod and continued. "Good, that leaves one single question to be answered. Do we go now, or do we stick with our original schedule? If the answer is now, we need to move on. The refuelling rocket needs to be topped up and launched at least eight hours ahead of Discovery." With his best poker face, he turned to face the President and stared into the cold, almost reptilian, eyes of the country's soulless head of state.

The President concluded the meeting with a single sentence. "Unless there are any objections, I give my consent to launching at the earliest possible time."

Laura glanced at her watch – she hadn't been on the ship for a whole day, and now she was about to be plucked off it by a helicopter. Laura was on the bridge meeting with the ship's captain. He was a slim, handsome man with a shaved head and sipped on a cup of Earl Grey tea. He could tell that Laura was apprehensive, perhaps even terrified, about what would transpire. And he didn't blame her one bit – what she was about to do was terrifying, not to mention very dangerous.

"So, you don't like being aboard our beautiful Diamond Princess?" Captain Stalway asked with a grin.

Laura responded. "There's nothing I would like to do more than stay on board this beautiful vessel, Captain. Well, that's not quite true; there is one thing..."

Laura proceeded to bring the captain up to date with her cover story and that the shuttle launch was being brought forward due to logistical reasons.

Impressed with Laura's reason, the captain nodded. "It's not going to be easy getting you off the ship. You may have noticed that we do not have a helipad. A couple of navy choppers will be along soon, and one will lower a harness that we will clip you into and winch you off the ship. Because of the importance of your leaving, I will speak with head office and see if we can arrange another cruise for you once you return from your next voyage. Pack your cases and leave them in your stateroom, and we'll get them sent to your home. Now we need to get you kitted out with some coveralls."

The captain had been more than understanding and helpful, not to mention impressed. Laura made her way to the Sky Deck, wearing baggy dark blue coveralls with a thick leather belt tied around her waist to prevent the wind from billowing them out. Two staff dressed in firefighting gear with full facemasks and respirators escorted her to the winch zone. The ship slowed from its cruising speed of 22 knots to five and had altered course so that there was little wind blowing across the deck. It was a balancing act – any slower meant the water swell became more of a problem, and any faster meant the wind became more dangerous. They were still some way from the coast, and on the Sky Deck, Laura scanned the sky for the Coast Guard helicopter. In the distance, she could hear the high-pitched drone of a turboprop aircraft and a couple of minutes later, she could make out the twin-engine HC-144 Ocean Sentry aircraft against the clear blue sky. The white plane with a dayglow orange tail and livery stripes orbited the cruise ship at an altitude of under a thousand feet. Apparently, the ship was close to the maximum range the rescue helicopter could fly and complete the transfer, so the turboprop acted as an intermediary. The pilot of the plane liaised with the ship's crew so that the helicopter could spend minimal time transferring the passenger. After about twenty minutes, the aircraft increased altitude, but they kept orbiting the cruise ship. The helicopter came into view, completed an inspection of the vessel and hovered into place above the winch zone.

The ship's first engineer was the resident expert on helicopter transfers, and he escorted Laura to the winch zone, now cleared of deck chairs and passengers. Laura was unaware of everyone watching her from every available vantage point. Several people had their phones, cameras and camcorders recording the event, and many were muttering about the reason for her departure. Was she an international criminal or someone in need of emergency medical assistance? Gossip was rife and sure to reverberate around the ship for the remainder of the cruise.

Laura felt weak at the knees as she looked at the helicopter hovering 60 feet or so above her. The thumping of the blades and the force of the downdraft were terrifying. She watched as the helicopter's crew lowered the harness.

"Step back, ma'am." the engineer requested. "There's likely to be a significant static charge on the end of that harness that could knock you flying. We need the harness to touch the deck first to ground to the same state as the ship."

Laura nodded and appreciated the advice when she saw a crisp blue flash as the harness kissed the deck. Fortunately, the seas were relatively calm, and the wind made for an effortless transfer. The engineer grabbed and unclipped the harness and helped Laura step into it. Attaching it back to the wire rope, he shouted to Laura to keep her arms close to her chest and to lock her ankles together until she was well inside the helicopter. Again, Laura kept quiet and just gave a nod of acknowledgement. With a final tap on her shoulder, the engineer stepped back, looked up and gave two thumbs up to the winch operator. Laura felt her weight reduce, suddenly realising she was no longer on the deck. The helicopter rose gently and moved out over the water to avoid any possible collision or entanglement with the ship. Laura switched her gaze from down to up and back again – the ship got smaller, and the helicopter larger. She felt exhilarated, liberated. Within a few seconds, she felt a powerful arm drag her into the safety of the helicopter's cabin, which was already heading at full speed towards the mainland. Donning noise-cancelling headphones, Laura listened as the helicopter's pilot informed her that an F15 jet was waiting to take her to Florida. Flying at altitude and with a speed above Mach 2, her flight was sure to annoy many people on the ground, but it was the fastest way to get her to the launch site.

# Chapter Twenty Two

Brad Sommers was in Mission Control stationed at one of the General Use Systems – a complex computer system sporting several flat-panel displays to monitor and manage any aspect of a launch programme. Brad watched the live video feeds from Launch Pads 39A and 39B. The modified fuel tank assembly sat on Pad 39A. Originally planned to employ a Delta IV Heavy, technical problems led to a change in plan. The refuelling rocket now comprised a standard external space shuttle fuel tank with six solid rocket boosters attached in two clusters. The Space Shuttle Discovery gleamed in the autumnal sunlight on pad 39B. Crews were working overtime on both rockets, and fuelling operations were in full swing, as evidenced by the wisps of cryogenic gases venting out of the top of the main fuel tanks. A third monitor displayed the status of the two launch pads. The board showed solid amber for both 39A and 39B, indicating that the launch areas were hazardous but could be entered cautiously. The light for Pad 39C remained off. Brad managed a chuckle over this. Although installed with warning lights, Launch Pad 39C did not exist. The Kennedy Space Centre was celebrating its 50th year and, during that time, had seen the comings and goings of the Mercury, Gemini, Apollo, Skylab and Shuttle programmes and not to mention numerous military and other unmanned probe launches. However, it never actually needed the additional launch pad. He guessed that 50 years ago, few would have imagined that the interest in space exploration would wane so quickly. The space shuttle's development was well underway when the Kennedy Space Centre celebrated its 15th year; in real terms, little had happened since then. Brad recalled a line from the movie 'The Right Stuff' – 'No bucks, no Buck Rogers.'

Putting on a thin wireless headset, Brad selected a contact name from a drop-down menu on one of the screens. "Hi, Dave, Brad here.

Can you please give me a fuelling status update for both vehicles?"

After a few seconds came a reply, "No problems so far, Brad, both hydrogen and lox tanks are filling up nicely, and the pressurisation curves are all nominal. I expect to finish in three to three and a half hours."

Brad thanked him for the information and diverted his attention to a screen that displayed the schematics for the flying fuel tank. It was a jury-rigged solution Brad had helped to design, but he still held concerns that the four additional solid rocket boosters, or SRBs, would place too much stress on the main tank. More importantly, if the engines were not balanced properly, they would cause the whole assembly to spin out of control with devastating results. On a shuttle launch, the three liquid fuel main engines at the back of the shuttle (the SSMEs) provide both thrust and steering control. Thousands of times a second, sensors on the shuttle would monitor the stresses on the frame caused by any variances between the two solid rocket boosters and compensate accordingly by making small changes in the attitude of the SSMEs. When the need for a flying fuel tank became apparent, the first hurdle was handling the steering problem. In an SRB, the fuel and oxidiser are stored in the same rubbery compound, which burns to exhaustion once ignited. Unlike a liquid fuel rocket, you cannot turn off or throttle down a solid rocket booster.

When the Delta IV Heavy option became untenable, the engineers decided to jury rig another shuttle assembly sans the actual shuttle. The original proposal for an orbital refuelling station involved attaching modified SRBs to an external space shuttle fuel tank. However, a standard SRB has a burn duration of just over two minutes, but at least 6 minutes of continuous thrust is needed to inject the rocket into a low Earth orbit. After investigating many scenarios, the engineers concluded that an SRB-only solution was not a viable option. Neither were the options of sending up a second shuttle or building a new delivery system from scratch considered plausible. The solution ultimately developed involved six solid rocket boosters, instead of two, and a cluster of three SSMEs and orbital manoeuvring engines housed on a bare frame. Orbital steering was to be provided by small retro-rocket packs at strategic points along the lengthened external fuel tank. The additional SRBs would allow the assembly to reach orbit sooner, but it would experience g-forces much greater than that associated with normal shuttle launches. But as this launch was unmanned, this would not prove an issue.

On a laptop he had brought with him into Mission Control, Brad opened some engineering software and entered some figures listed on the booster assembly schematics displayed on the screen in front of him. He smiled when he saw the results. The numbers still made sense and the engineers had more than accounted for the additional stresses on the assembly. All he had to worry about now was whether or not the SRBs would work to specification, augmenting the steering control of the SSMEs. Considering a problem with an SRB had led to the death of the seven astronauts and the loss of the space shuttle Challenger in 1986, Brad remained a little apprehensive. He felt somewhat comforted that no lives would be lost if it didn't work. Then, on the flip side, it would mean that they would not get back to the Moon for two years or more. They would have missed their chance, and the Chinese would have won. Whatever they find in the lunar structure may have far-reaching consequences that could influence the dynamics of geopolitics. They may even discover technologies to make them supreme leaders of the entire planet – a disturbing thought that Brad dreaded but could not shake off.

Laura sat in the navigator's seat directly behind the F-15E's pilot. Her flight suit was uncomfortable, and the air in the cockpit was stale and filled with the scent of oil, industrial solvents and other carcinogens. It wasn't the 'Top Gun' sophistication she expected, Laura thought as she scanned the well-worn controls around her. This plane must be at least 25 years old, she guessed. As part of her fast-tracked astronaut training, Laura had experienced several flights in one of NASA's near-new and shiny T-38s, a twin-engine supersonic trainer built by Northrop and based on the airframe of the F-5 combat fighter. In this trainer, she had learnt how to handle high g-forces using techniques like gritting her teeth and clenching her toes, buttocks and abdomen. Her thoughts were interrupted by the sudden sensation of being pushed forward. The aircraft was decelerating. She looked at the instrument panel and noted that they were already under Mach 1, and the aircraft was still slowing. Their altitude had also dropped significantly – Laura could no longer make out the curvature of the Earth, and the ground had lost much of its fuzzy blue tinge. To get the plane to fly as fast as possible, they had climbed close to its service ceiling of 65,000 feet – where the air is noticeably thinner. They were now flying at just 15,000 feet, well below the cruising altitude of commercial passenger aircraft. She heard the pilot's update in her headphones: "Dropping to refuelling altitude – the 135 is five miles to our 12."

Laura acknowledged the update and noted the blip on her radar panel up ahead. For some reason, she found the pilot somewhat aloof and grumpy. Everything that needed to be done to get her to the Cape appeared too much of an inconvenience for him. As a result, the flight had been a quiet one. At one stage, Laura had to think hard even to recall his name.

Laura sat in silence as the F-15E approached the KC-135 Strato-tanker. She wished she could hear the conversation between the pilot and the refuelling tanker; however, the pilot had switched her headset off. She looked around the control panels and found a switch for communications but decided not to fiddle with it. The last thing she wanted to do was to piss off an already pissed-off pilot, especially during such a delicate and dangerous procedure. Instead, she watched as the pilot expertly manoeuvred the aircraft into position behind the tanker. She heard the door to the refuelling probe open and a gentle whirling noise as the probe extended and clicked into place. Now directly behind and below the KC-135 and less than 50 feet away, Laura could see the refuelling boom extend from the back of the tanker. The boom had two little winglets with workable control surfaces, and the refuelling officer aboard the KC-135 eased the end of the boom towards the F-15's fuel probe. At the same time, the pilot manoeuvred the probe towards the boom. A few seconds passed, and an audible 'clunk' signalled the successful mating of the two aircraft. Seconds later, the sound of gushing fuel filled the cockpit, and the nearly-depleted tanks were replenished. The noise was reminiscent of a flushing toilet. It felt to Laura that it was already over as soon as it had begun. The tanker's boom detached from the fighter's probe, and the refuelling tanker began to gain altitude and turn to the left. The fighter maintained its altitude for a few seconds before engaging full thrust, albeit without afterburners, and then began a steep climb. Passing through 40,000 feet, the pilot engaged the afterburners to push the Strike Eagle through Mach 1 and close to Mach 2. Levelling out at 60,000 feet, the pilot increased the speed until the dial read Mach 2.3. Back to the Cape soon, Laura thought. She took one more look at the distinct curvature of the Earth and realised that in the next couple of days – barring accident or disaster – she would see the whole planet as an entire disk. Laura closed her eyes and did not open them until she was on the final approach.

# Chapter Twenty Four

September 17, 2012, Kennedy Space Flight Centre, FL

Less than two hours after landing, Laura was in the observation room of Mission Control in the same clothes she was wearing on the cruise ship. She desperately needed a shower, a change of clothes, and a lie-down. It was nearly midnight, and she was exhausted – not to mention hungry. Laura watched through the glass as thirty or so people sat at workstations. Some were doing nothing except staring at the large displays on the far wall. Others typed at their keyboards – all wore thin wireless headsets. Laura spied Brad at one of the terminals – she had never seen him look so professional. His trademark smile was gone, and the look of concentration could be seen on his brow – he was immersed in his job. The clock had stopped at 73 seconds. One of the systems had triggered a warning light, and the countdown halted automatically. That was over 15 minutes ago. The activation light for Pad 39A flashed amber, indicating that there were people on the launch pad, but no other vehicles should approach. A few more minutes passed, and Laura noticed on one of the screens that a truck had left the launch pad. The activation light switched from flashing amber to solid red. A minute later, the countdown resumed: 72, 71, 70… As is tradition, as soon as the countdown hit 60, a human voice added to the countdown.

"Sixty seconds to launch of Omega II Alpha, Van Allen's long endurance experiment, signalling NASA's preparation for our return to the Moon and eventually to Mars. Fifty seconds and counting." The voice continued, "30 seconds, and the board is clean. At 15 seconds, we reach the commit phase, 20 seconds, 19, 18, 17, 16… We are committed to launching, igniters firing up, 14, 13, 12, 11, 10, 9…"

A shower of sparks sprayed into the area directly below the SSMEs. The exhaust cones shuddered, and crisp blue jets of flame appeared. Seconds later, the six solid rocket boosters ignited in unison.

The impulse imparted by such thrust caused the whole rocket assembly to shudder and shake. Kilometres away from the launch pad, Laura could feel the ground rumble under the sheer power of the rockets. In a matter of seconds, all six SRBs produced their maximum rated thrust.

"2, 1, lift-off." The explosive bolts which held the rocket to the launch pad detonated, and the rocket began to rise. Everyone in the control room sat in silence as the rocket cleared the tower, powered skyward and began its roll towards the east. The unmanned rocket climbed much faster than the space shuttle or even the gargantuan Apollo 5 rockets of the 60s and early 70s. Looking at the board, Laura noticed it was pulling a little over eight g's – over twice the g-force she would experience aboard the space shuttle Discovery.

Several long focal-length lenses tracked the rocket's path as it thundered across the night sky. At T+133 seconds the six almost exhausted SRBs separated from the main assembly like enormous fireworks and fell away for parachute landings in the Atlantic Ocean. The SSMEs continued to burn for the next few minutes until the payload attained a successful orbit.

The tension in Mission Control was replaced with cheers and laughter when their scientists confirmed the rocket's orbit. The first and possibly most tenuous stage of an ambitious flight programme had concluded without a hitch. Brad's usual relaxed smile returned, and he turned to see Laura in the observation area. He waved to her, gave her two thumbs up and blew her a kiss. She blew a kiss in reply, and with a broad smile, she took a deep breath as the realisation hit her – nothing will stop her from going to the Moon now.

# Chapter Twenty Five

21 September 2012, Space Shuttle Discovery

Laura was on her back, "sitting" in the port Mission Specialist seat within the Space Shuttle Discovery. She was positioned behind and between the Pilot's and Commander's seats and had an excellent view out of the shuttle's two front windows. Next to her sat Mission Specialist Darryl Candy, who sported a smile that would put the Cheshire Cat to shame. They looked at each other through their bulky helmets and exchanged a nod and grin. It was clear to Laura that they were sharing the same emotions – excitement tainted with pure adrenalin-filled fear. In unison, they looked back towards the front of the shuttle. All Laura could see was a brilliant blue sky with a hint of wispy cirrus cloud through the window.

Three days late, she thought to herself, three whole days! They had lost critical time because of a faulty micro-switch in one of the many redundant backup systems. During that time, NASA's tracking facilities monitored the progress of the Chinese craft as it entered trans-lunar trajectory, successfully established orbit and finally landed men on the surface just a few kilometres away from the structure. For the first time in just shy of 40 years, humanity had returned to the Moon – yet few on Earth knew. For the first time in history, the footprints on the lunar regolith were not those of an American. The NSA was busy trying to decrypt the radio communications between the astronauts and Chinese ground control, but they had been unsuccessful so far. However, given the amount of radio traffic intercepted, it was clear that the Chinese programme was running to schedule. Laura watched as Discovery's Pilot and Commander went through their checklists, ensuring that all switches and knobs were correctly set and that one of the most complex machines conceived and created by man was ready for launch. She glanced at the launch clock; it was stopped at T-9 minutes. Nothing terrible had happened. It was a routine checkpoint in the countdown sequence.

Laura looked at a monitor to her left. It showed the helmeted outlines of the three crew members stationed in the mid-deck area almost directly below her. All three shared the same look as Candy, and she wondered if they felt any better or worse for being harnessed in a windowless compartment. In the port seat sat Brian Paris, an expert in exobiology. Initially, she wondered how anyone could be an exobiology expert as no extra-terrestrial life had ever been discovered – publicly, at least if the conspiracy theorists were correct. However, after looking up the term on the Internet, she found that this field of research also dealt with the effects of extra-terrestrial surroundings on living organisms – including humans. Sitting next to him in the centre seat was the bubbly astronaut and mission specialist Jamie Harting. Although born in England, Jamie had spent most of her life in Texas and became naturalised when her parents became citizens. More American than apple pie, Jamie had never managed to lose her coarse cockney accent even though her relatives in England thought she sounded so American. Kurt Limberg, the crew's quiet and reflective payload specialist, occupied the starboard seat. Kurt had served on three previous shuttle missions, but one would not have realised this by the look on his face – he shared the same look of excitement, anguish and helplessness as the rest of the passengers aboard Discovery. Clearly, there was nothing routine about a space shuttle launch.

A conversation with Brad from a year ago suddenly came to Laura's mind. She became acutely aware that she was sitting atop a thousand tonnes of solid rocket propellant and over two million litres of liquid fuel. Light blue touch paper and retire, she mused as she recalled the instructions on the fireworks Laura used to launch with her father when she was a little girl. She tried to take her mind off the immediate present. Laura squeezed her eyes closed and tried to visualise where she would be if she were still on her cruise. Laura imagined herself on the big cruise ship's deck, watching the glaciers crack, break up and calve into College Fjord, Alaska.

"T-9 minutes: the count has resumed, and GLS auto sequence has commenced." The voice over the intercom signalled that the countdown had resumed.

The Pilot and Commander were busy with their tasks, but in the Mission Specialist's seat, Laura had nothing to do but wait. She felt bloated and clumsy in her Advanced Crew Escape Suit, or ACES – more lovingly known as a pumpkin suit. Adrenalin built up in her system – her brain processed her environment much faster than usual. Seconds appeared to tick by slowly as if time was affected by some strange relativistic effect.

Updates from Mission Control kept coming through the intercom: "Retract orbiter access arm... perform APU pre-start... go for APU start... close lox inboard F and D valve... open lox drain valve..."

A lump formed in Laura's throat as she heard an important message from mission control. 'T minus one minute.' This could be her last minute on Earth should something go wrong with the launch. Laura looked at the Commander and Pilot and noticed they were no longer doing anything – both had their arms folded across their chests. The shuttle was now running in a fully automatic mode.

Mission control's commentary continued. "T minus 6 seconds, main engine start... 5, 4, 3, SRB ignition, 2, 1, and lift off of Discovery on the Omega II mission."

The ignition of the main shuttle engines was gentle compared to the raw and coarse thrust of the solid rocket boosters. Discovery shook, and Laura felt a gut-wrenching twang as the explosive bolts blew, separating the rocket from the launch pad. The g-forces built up quickly but smoothly, forcing the crew into their seats. Laura tried to lift her arms against the high g-forces; although it was possible, she realised it took a lot of effort. No wonder much of the launch process was automated. Now and then, the pilot entered a four-character command into the flight computer to begin the next phase of the launch program – however, even this took a lot of strength. Laura now felt the whole shuttle begin to twist – this was the roll procedure where the shuttle rotated 180 degrees around its long axis so that it was upside down relative to the ground but with a pitch of 78 degrees from horizontal. The shuttle was now flying towards the east and was taking advantage of the angular momentum of Earth's rotation to enjoy a supersonic boost into orbit.

Laura's heart continued to race. She was disappointed that she could see nothing but blue sky out of the window – however, she noticed that the sky had become noticeably darker as Discovery powered its way through the atmosphere. She checked the mission clock– less than 40 seconds had passed since launch, and then she heard the Pilot speak to mission control.

"Throttle back," the pilot said.

Laura acutely knew what this meant. They reduced the thrust from the shuttle's main engines while it passed through the so-called Max-Q phase – the period during which the whole shuttle assembly endures maximum dynamic stresses placed upon it and is when something catastrophic is most likely to happen, as it did during the ill-fated Challenger mission STS-51L on that cold winter's morning in January 1986. Not so much a design flaw as a product used out of acceptable parameters. A simple composite rubber sea, called an O-ring, on one of the solid rocket boosters had become too brittle in the unusually cold weather and had subsequently failed. Super-heated exhaust gasses breached the seal, which worked like a blow torch against the thin and unprotected underbelly of the shuttle's main fuel tank. The external fuel tank is the only non-reusable component of the space shuttle and has no heat shield as it is designed to burn up in the atmosphere. The jet of white-hot plasma that bypassed the compromised seal took mere seconds to pierce the thin skin of the fuel tank. Hundreds of tonnes of fuel and oxidiser exploded, and Challenger broke up and fell back to Earth. The entire crew of seven perished, including Christa McAuliffe, a school teacher who was to be the first civilian in space. The space shuttle program changed the perception of space travel from specialised high-risk ventures into routine journeys not much different to a commercial airline flight. NASA had become too complacent, resulting in the loss of Challenger and seven brave souls. Laura was too young to remember the actual explosion. However, at school, she had to write a term paper on the American space program, and she had watched a documentary on video that had impacted her as if she had witnessed the disaster first-hand. With her eyes tightly closed, Laura recalled the eerie cloud formed by the shuttle Challenger on that eventful day. The routine trail of the shuttle's ascent, the bloated body at the point of the explosion and the tendrils of smoke that outlined the wreckage path as it fell back to Earth. It hung in the air as a warning of all the dangers that explorers face. It reminded Laura of a grotesque sea creature – a jellyfish or man o'war.

"Go for throttle up." The pilot commented.

Seventy-three seconds Laura thought – the time at which Challenger exploded. The three g's of force the engines exerted on her body amplified her sense of dread. Again, she closed her eyes as tightly as possible and wondered what the mission doctor thought as he evaluated the telemetry from the medical sensors she wore.

Fortunately, the shuttle passed through the period of Max-Q without incident. The sky lost even more of its blue as the shuttle raced further into space.

The crew experienced a moderate jolt forward two minutes into the flight as if the pilot had momentarily stomped on the brakes. The solid rocket boosters had separated from the large external fuel tank. A combination of explosive bolts and small rocket motors had pushed these away from the shuttle before they had completely exhausted their fuel.

Without the solid rocket boosters, Laura didn't feel any noticeable loss of g-force as the shuttle's main engines adjusted their thrust accordingly. However, the flight had suddenly become much smoother and far less noisy. Instead of feeling that she was driving on a dirt track in a big clunky SUV, she now had the sensation of cruising on a smooth, tarmacked surface in a high-performance sports car.

I'm actually in space! Laura realised as she looked through the front window. Any hint of the blue life-giving nitrogen-oxygen atmosphere was gone; all she could see now was the inky blackness of space. There was too much light in the cockpit to see any stars, but Laura was looking forward to seeing the Milky Way's full majesty as the shuttle made its way around the planet's dark side.

With the adrenalin of the launch metabolising in her body, Laura noticed that the final few minutes of the shuttle's flight into low Earth orbit passed surprisingly quickly. She felt a rapid deceleration as the shuttle's main engines throttled down and didn't even feel the main fuel tank detach. Laura then felt one of the strangest sensations she had ever experienced. To her, it was as if her brain and stomach were floating within her body. She felt incredibly light-headed. She was weightless and, along with her six crewmates and the shuttle, was falling to Earth as rapidly as Earth rotated. She giggled when she thought about the number of people who mistakenly believed that Earth's gravity magically switches off in space. Laura knew that Earth still exhibited a force of gravity – how else did the Moon stay in orbit? However, by virtue of the shuttle's lateral velocity, they were essentially in constant free-fall around the Earth – hence weightless but still under the influence of Earth's substantial gravitational field.

"Mission control, this is Discovery – main SMEs throttled down, and successful main tank separation acknowledged, over." Pilot Rod Hoey communicated to mission control in a calm, rock-steady voice.

"We copy that Discovery. We have a green board down here, and LEO insertion burn is scheduled at T plus 45 minutes. Over," came the reply.

"Roger that. Over and out."

With that, the pilot and commander removed their helmets and did the 10 seconds of customary play with them in zero-g. Lance Halas, the shuttle's Hispanic commander, then unfastened his harness and pushed himself out of his seat. Effortlessly he dragged himself towards Laura and Darryl Candy.

"You can unharness now, guys and get out of these pumpkin suits," Halas said to Laura and Darryl. "Just be careful not to knock any switches and keep a sick bag with you just in case. The vomit comet only lasts a minute at a time – we'll be weightless for considerably longer than that."

Wriggling out of a space suit is relatively easy on Earth, but it proves to be more of a challenge when weightless. After several seconds of trying, Laura noticed that she was upside down in relation to the shuttle and its occupants. Judging by the expletives emanating from Darryl, it appeared that he was having similar problems.

A flash! Was there a problem? Laura thought. She turned to see the pilot Rod Hoey taking a photo of her on his smartphone.

"That's one for the books," Rod chuckled. "I remember my first time getting out of a pumpkin suit – not a pretty sight. May I suggest you help each other? Alternatively, wrap your ankles around the seat's headrest to get some purchase." Rod returned to work and prepared the shuttle for low Earth orbit insertion.

Somewhat embarrassed, Darryl and Laura followed Rod's suggestion and managed to get out of the pumpkin suits without much further difficulty. Darryl offered to take Laura's suit and helmet to the storage area, which she gratefully accepted. This provided Laura with an opportunity to look around the cockpit. She could see sunlight through the cargo bay windows as the large clam-shell doors slowly opened. The cargo bay doors on the space shuttle serve two primary purposes. It obviously allows cargo to be taken out of and put into the shuttle bay. The network of pipes embedded into the payload doors was less obvious but just as important. These allow excess heat the orbiter generates to be radiated into space, saving the crew from a slow, painful death through heat exhaustion. Laura gasped as she saw her first glimpses of the Earth from space. In her excitement, she dragged herself to the observation window in the cockpit's ceiling and saw the most beautiful site she had ever seen. They were flying over the Atlantic Ocean, and the African continent was about to come into view. The muted colour of blue and brown took her breath away. She couldn't see any signs of life – the atmosphere all but filtered out the green hues of vegetation – nor could she make out any man-made features. Apart from the well-known shape of the continent, she could easily be passing over some barren and desolate alien landscape. It was hard to conceive that there were around seven billion people on that planet – eating, sleeping, working and going through their daily routines, not to mention the countless billions of other creatures doing their things. She angled her head back as far as she could. There it was – the thin band of atmosphere that gave Earth all of its life.

Fifty minutes had elapsed since lift-off, and a burn of the main engines had just lifted the orbiter into a stable low Earth orbit – one that would catch up with the refuelling rocket in a little over four and a half hours. Lance Halas, the shuttle's commander, was in discussion with Mission Control. Laura noticed that his face was stern – his eyes deep in thought. Lance muttered a few words and switched off the communication circuit.

"Anything wrong?" Laura asked.

"Not with us. Just after our launch, the NSA noticed a change in radio traffic from Chinese ground control to their astronauts. At first, they thought our launch had put them into a state of radio silence. However, they have rejected this reason as it will take us almost five days to get to the Moon. It now appears that all radio traffic is one-way from the Earth to the Moon, and all communications from the Chinese astronauts have ceased." Lance replied as he rubbed his hand through his shortly cropped hair.

"Comms malfunction?" Laura suggested.

"Possibly, however, Mission Control has asked me to think about rescue options should it be something more… disastrous. We have no idea how many people they have on the surface or in lunar orbit. Based on what we know about their space programme, we estimate between three and five astronauts in total. I must work out how to accommodate these astronauts should the need arise. The nerds at Mission Control are going to work out if it is even possible based on the load their presence will place on our oxygen, water and food stores. The LRO is to be re-tasked to see what's happening on the surface. Keep your fingers crossed that it shows everything OK down there – otherwise, our mission may be seriously compromised." Although talking to Laura, Lance's piercing blue eyes stared into the distance. Already he was mentally going through the possible scenarios he may face and was thinking up possible solutions to each.

# Chapter Twenty-Six

Darryl Candy was a large man. He was technically too large to be an astronaut at just over six feet tall and of stocky build. However, he was the designer and chief engineer of the refuelling rocket assembly and was considered the only person with the necessary skills required to supervise the shuttle's docking to it and to fix any problems should they arise. He was kitted out in his space suit, formally known as an Extravehicular Mobility Unit – EMU for short – and was checking the integrity of its seals. Also geared up in an EMU suit was Payload Commander Kurt Limberg. Although he had a Germanic name, Kurt had an Asian origin. Born in Vietnam, he had been orphaned in his home country after the Vietnam War had concluded. Found abandoned and close to death, he was rescued by a couple who brought him back to health, took him to the USA and ultimately adopted him as their own. While floating in the small airlock with Darryl, Kurt continued his pre-breathing routine to purge any remaining nitrogen from his bloodstream and body tissue. Darryl gave Kurt the thumbs up, and Kurt reciprocated.

"Bring suit pressure up to atmosphere plus 29.6 kilopascals. Airlock oxygen disabled," Darryl said over his suit's intercom.

The two astronauts felt their suits balloon out, and their ears popped as they slowly increased the pressure. Once at the assigned pressure, they watched their chest-mounted digital display looking for any significant leaks. Darryl's suit read 0.02kpa per minute drop, and Kurt's was somewhat higher at 0.08kpa per minute – both well below the maximum allowed loss of 1.38kpa per minute.

"All good," Darryl said. "Airlock oxygen on, depressurise suit to ambient."

Within a few minutes, their suits equalised to the pressure of the airlock, and with their suit integrity confirmed, Darryl activated the pump to evacuate the atmosphere from the airlock. As the air purged from the chamber, Darryl and Kurt gradually reduced the pressure in their suits and continued their pre-breathing exercises. After half an hour, the airlock was close to a pure vacuum and Darryl, and Kurt's suits were at one-third normal atmospheric pressure. The pressure differential made their suits stiff, and it took additional effort for Darryl to grip the handle to open the airlock door to the shuttle's cargo bay. As he turned the lever, the remaining air in the chamber vaporised into a thin cloud that leaked into the infinity of space.

Darryl was the first to exit the airlock. Grabbing a handrail, he pulled himself into the cargo bay and swivelled around. He then helped Kurt out and closed and sealed the door behind them. Hand over hand, they made their way to the two Manned Manoeuvring Units or MMUs. These small self-contained jet packs allow untethered astronauts to move freely around the shuttle's exterior. As the MMUs provide such a low thrust, only a rudimentary nylon harness with a plastic clip was required to secure an astronaut to the unit.

Before they detached from the shuttle, the astronauts tested the MMU's 24 thrusters to ensure that all the gas-powered units worked as expected. Should just one of the thrusters stick open, it would result in uncontrollable manoeuvrability of the astronaut with potentially disastrous results. Satisfied that all was in order, Darryl and Kurt exited the shuttle bay and headed towards the fuel/booster assembly at a fast-walking pace.

Like on the Moon, the lack of atmosphere in a low Earth orbit makes it difficult to judge distances. An appreciation of the apparent size of the refuelling rocket was the only way to gauge how far they were away from it. On their way, Kurt used the spin thrusters to look back at the shuttle while still approaching the refuelling rocket. With a modified Nikon digital SLR camera, he took several photos of Discovery as it hung impossibly in the void. Reorienting to his travelling direction, he took a few more pictures, this time of the refuelling rocket with the west coast of Africa in the background. Within a few minutes, Darryl and Kurt were at the refuelling rocket. Although the astronauts could not hear the thrusters in the vacuum of space, they felt them 'pop' as they delivered small but precise impulse quanta.

The two astronauts inspected the booster assembly for any signs of damage – luckily, there were none. Kurt then moved to a small access panel on the side of the booster and used a large T-bar hexagonal key from his tool bag to open it. From behind the panel, Kurt extracted a small box connected to the booster assembly via a long electrical cable.

Kurt flicked a few switches on the box and radioed back to the shuttle that they were good to go for docking. Kurt began by rotating the refuelling rocket around its long axis so that the side of the fuel tank without the booster assembly faced towards Discovery. Aboard the shuttle, Rod Hoey watched the camera feed on a laptop in the cockpit. The barren side of the booster array was peppered with marker symbols that the software on his computer used to determine precisely the attitude of the refuelling rocket relative to Discovery. Below the image, the software displayed a set of manoeuvring instructions Hoey relayed to Kurt.

For twenty minutes, Kurt slowly nudged and jiggled the refuelling rocket towards Discovery. Taking control of the digital camera, Darryl had positioned himself about 250 metres away so he could photographically document the unique and delicate task as it unfolded in front of him.

Kurt continued the process of expertly aligning the refuelling rocket and nudged it ever closer to the shuttle. Even though his suit was liquid-cooled, the intense concentration required for this delicate mission-critical task caused sweat to build up on his brow. His 'Snoopy' cap would soak up most of his perspiration, but even in freefall, some of the sweat made its way into his eyes – the saline fluid stinging them.

The space shuttle is attached to the external fuel tank at three points – one towards the nose of the shuttle and two at the back. Usually, when the shuttle detaches from the tank, heat-shield tiles spring into place to protect the shuttle's underbelly from burning up when re-entering the atmosphere. However, a different mechanism was used for this launch to connect Discovery to the external fuel tank. Three stubs of the modified brackets stood proud from the shuttle's underbelly. These were gimballed and articulated to accommodate for some slack as flight stresses, and thermal expansion and compression in the harsh environment of space would make it difficult, if not impossible, to dock the shuttle to the tank using conventional fixed brackets.

Kurt was at the front of the shuttle and slowly guided the fuel tank's top bracket to the shuttle. Once aligned, Kurt took a large locking pin from his toolkit and inserted it into the frame. The shuttle was affixed to the refuelling/booster rocket at one location.

Now came the most dangerous part of the mission – connecting the umbilicals to Discovery. Kurt tapped a few buttons on the control panel, and the bottom of the external booster moved away from Discovery. Another tap, and the movement stopped. Kurt had just enough room to squeeze between the two craft, open the access port on the refuelling rocket and slowly pull out the fuel and control umbilicals toward the shuttle. If anything was to go wrong, then this was the time it was likely to happen. Being crushed between the two spacecraft was not Kurt's preferred method of meeting his maker. He swivelled around and opened a spring-loaded heat-shielded panel on Discovery. One-by-one Kurt attached the umbilicals. Each connector went in with no problems – it was all going better than planned.

"Discovery, EVA. Umbilicals are connected. Please confirm integrity, over." Kurt requested.

In the cockpit, Hoey pushed himself over to one of the control panels and flicked a series of switches on and off and looked at a bank of status lights as he did so. "EVA, Discovery. All looks good; job well done, over." He replied.

"Roger that Discovery, I'm now opening the valves, over."

Kurt accessed two valves on the external fuel tank that supplied propellant and oxidant to the shuttle's main engines. His heart almost stopped as the sudden flow of fluid caused the umbilicals to whip from side to side like an angry snake. He checked both ends of the umbilical to ensure nothing was venting into space. Happy that all was well, he manoeuvred back to the booster control panel.

On board Discovery, Hoey, now back at his laptop, continued to send attitude and distance information to Kurt. After ten more minutes of sweat-inducing concentration, the rear of the external tank was expertly aligned and secured to Discovery. Kurt made a final visit to each bracket and ensured that the gimballed connections were aligned correctly and locked into place.

"That's one hell of a job well done, Kurt." The voice of Darryl Candy came over his headset. "I've got some great stills and footage of the whole operation – you will be a global star, my friend."

"You always get the choice jobs, don't you, Darryl," Kurt replied with a laugh in his voice. He knew from the outset that it was a one-person task and that Darryl was there as a backup should he become incapacitated. "I'm heading back to the bay… care to join me?"

"I just want to take a few more pictures and enjoy the scenery – I will be with you in a few minutes."

Kurt deactivated the external control panel, secured it back into its compartment and moved about twenty metres away from Discovery. He spent a few moments observing the full majesty of the Earth as it passed beneath him.

The voice of Rod Hoey came over his headset, "Playtime's over, and night is coming up fast… time to come home."

###

At the height of the cold war, satellite communications became increasingly important and strategic. Placing satellites into orbit was expensive, and in the early years of the space age, it was also prone to catastrophic failure. Russia's solution for efficient communications over a given location was to use a single satellite placed into a so-called Molniya, or lightning, orbit. In a highly elliptical orbit inclined at over 60 degrees to the equator, a satellite in a Molniya orbit approaches Earth as close as 500km and as far out as 40,000km. A single satellite is within line-of-sight of its target location for as much as 90 per cent of its orbit. The other ten percent involves a whip-lash journey around the other side of the planet at speeds over 10 kilometres per second.

Launched in 1976, a Soviet tactical battlefield communications satellite placed in such an orbit had long since failed. Imperceptible atmospheric drag encountered every time the satellite approached its closest point to Earth built up, eventually leading to a catastrophic loss of orbit. With a faint streak of light in the night sky witnessed by only a few, the satellite met a fiery death as it burned up in the atmosphere, with a few small parts coming down over the South Pacific Ocean. However, during its few years of operation, a simple bolt had worked its way loose. Streamlined and not as burdened with the same atmospheric drag as the satellite, the bolt had continued on a gently decaying orbit for over 35 years. With odds that defy calculation, the trajectory of the bolt and that of Darryl Candy intersected spatially and temporally. Darryl died instantly as the projectile passed through his helmet and skull at a velocity eleven times that of a rifle bullet.

Pilot Rod Hoey was alerted to a problem when the sensors in Candy's suit sent out a hail of error and warning messages to the life-vitals station in the cockpit. Immediately he got onto the radio and tried in vain to contact Darryl.

On the open-mic system, Kurt overheard Rod's attempted communication and pitched 180 degrees – he immediately felt disoriented being upside down relative to Discovery. Another 180-degree rotation around a perpendicular axis brought him to a position that he could perceive as 'upright'. Kurt scanned the sky toward where Darryl was and panicked when he saw a small, still figure slowly rolling in the void. He applied thrust and made his way towards his colleague. Even though he was eager to get to him, Kurt was acutely aware of his hostile environment. Too much thrust would require proportionally more fuel to slow down. He only had a finite supply of this, which was already more than half exhausted.

As Kurt approached Darryl, he could see that something significant had happened. He was tumbling, but none of the MMU thrusters appeared to be stuck open. The astronauts and the shuttle headed into the night, and the amount of light dropped appreciably in a very short time. Kurt switched on the two halogen lights attached to his MMU and lifted his sun-glare visor. He was within 20 metres of his fellow astronaut when he noticed that Darryl's helmet didn't look right. A sense of dread consumed his gut, and Kurt instinctively slowed his approach. Bile rose in his throat as he realised what he was seeing. He struggled not to vomit. The entire front of Darryl's helmet was missing, as was most of his face. Manoeuvring within arm's length, Kurt hit the auto-orient button on Darryl's MMU. A series of micro-jets fired, and within a few seconds, Darryl's body was no longer tumbling. The sense of nausea returned as Kurt reviewed the scene. He could make out vapour wisps as the fluids, which were once part of Darryl, boiled off into the vacuum of space. Crystallised blood and brain matter coated the inside of what remained of his helmet. Kurt saw the small hole at the back of Darryl's helmet, which was a giveaway as to what had happened. He opened up communications to Discovery.

"Discovery, Kurt here. I'm with Darryl – he's dead. It's not a pretty sight. It looks like he's been hit by a micro-meteor or something, over."

The five other astronauts were on the flight deck to hear the devastating news. Tears welled in Laura's eyes – she looked around to see that she was not alone. With a sense of guilt, her scientist's brain kicked in as she observed that tears did not behave as she expected in a weightless environment. Instead of her teardrops floating off into the cabin, they adhered to her face. Something to do with surface tension, no doubt, Laura thought. Her mind returned to the present and the disaster.

Kurt came over the radio again, "Discovery, do you copy over?"

Rod Hoey, in apparent shock, tapped his comms button and acknowledged Kurt's transmission. "Can you bring him back to Discovery, over?" Hoey responded in a deflated tone. Swallowing hard, he continued, "We don't have the facilities to store a body within the shuttle, so we… uh… we will need to stow him in the payload bay. You will need to cover his body so that he doesn't receive any direct sunlight. That way, the coldness of space will prevent any decomposition, over."

Kurt acknowledged and proceeded to connect his safety tether to Darryl's MMU. The rope was designed especially for the event that a fellow astronaut, or his MMU, had become incapacitated. It was long enough so that the jets from the other would not have a significant effect on the astronaut under tow. This, in turn, produced its own set of unique problems when it came to manoeuvring in a weightless environment. Should the towing astronaut slow down, they ran the risk of being hit by the other astronaut. So, the towing astronaut had to move to the side when changing velocity. Without friction in space, the incapacitated astronaut would not slow down but would overtake the towing astronaut. As the rope tightened, the towing astronaut would whip around 180 degrees. It was like watching a slinky spring make its way down a flight of stairs.

With precision and patience, Kurt brought the remains of Darryl back to the shuttle bay. First, he extracted Darryl's lifeless body from the MMU and attached Darryl's suit to a safety cable. After stowing their MMUs back in their allotted places, Kurt made his way to an equipment locker hand-over-hand and retrieved a reflective Mylar sheet and several lengths of webbing. With tears of grief stinging his eyes, he worked in silence. He wrapped the body in the flimsy sheet as best he could and then secured it to an equipment frame with the webbing. Completely exhausted physically and emotionally, Kurt made his way back to the airlock.

# Chapter Twenty-Seven

Laura floated in near foetal position in the mid-deck. Her cheeks were still wet with tears, and her nose was red with grief. She flicked her finger across the screen on her tablet computer, and another page of Richard Fairbrother's notes appeared. Nothing in them made any real sense about what had just happened. To be alive one second and gone the next was something Laura found hard to conceive. All that was once a jovial Darryl Candy was gone save for the inanimate collection of dead cells, fibres and mineralised bone that remained. Another incongruous thought – the essence of a person is something that any physical quantity cannot define. Is there a soul? Does it persist after death? If so, where does it go? These thoughts, which have no answer after millennia of human existence, overwhelmed Laura. She sobbed some more.

The internal door of the airlock opened, and with helmet and camera in one hand, Kurt pulled himself into the mid-deck cabin with his other. His face was gaunt and sweaty – his hair pasted to his forehead.

"Help me out of this thing, please, Laura," Kurt mumbled.

Laura let go of her tablet, pushed over to Kurt and helped him wriggle out of the suit. Kurt's blue flight coveralls were drenched in sweat – he was exhausted and in shock. Laura went to the galley, extracted a cold electrolytic drink pack, and passed it to him. They floated in silence while he finished sipping on his drink. Together they made their way towards the flight deck, where the rest of the crew discussed the situation.

Kurt pulled himself up the ladder and onto the flight deck, receiving pats on the back from the crew. There were few smiles, however, as all were still coming to terms with the death of Darryl Candy. Lance Halas, the shuttle's commander, separated from the others and continued his quiet discussion with Mission Control.

After a few minutes, Lance removed his headset and called for the crew's attention. With his usual calm voice, he recounted his discussion with Mission Control. "First, I would like to take a few minutes to silently pray for the soul of our colleague and good friend Darryl Candy. Without his drive, intellect and humour, we would not be on this mission today."

Everyone bowed their heads and spent a minute reflecting on their loss. Laura thought about Darryl's wife, now a widow, and her three-year-old son, who was now fatherless. Had she been told yet? What would she be feeling, and how would she explain the situation to her son? Sadness engulfed her.

Lance continued, "As you know, I have spent some time talking with Mission Control. Firstly, the mission is to continue as planned. As you are aware, before we commenced this mission, we all provided NASA with updated wills. It appears that Darryl's requested a lunar 'burial' should he die on the way to the Moon. Mission Control granted his request as he was due to be part of the landing party and because two of us must remain on the shuttle. The reason for this is a rather macabre one, as Darryl's body will act as ballast so that the moonhopper behaves as expected. The regolith is too thin for a proper burial – not that we have the gear for digging a grave – so we will have to devise a compromise solution. On another matter, Mission Control has been monitoring the Chinese traffic to and from the Moon. Less than an hour ago, all communications from the Chinese ground station ceased. There have been no signals from the Chinese astronauts since just after we launched. It appears that the Chinese Space Agency has abandoned its mission, and we must assume that they consider their astronauts lost. What we must consider is the reason for the loss of communications. Is it due to a technical problem with their equipment, or does it have something to do with the lunar structure itself? Did the Chinese astronauts encounter unfriendly aliens? We simply do not know. Regardless, we need to focus on our mission. We need to prepare for Trans-Lunar Insertion. With the loss of Darryl, Mission Control has decided to put TLI off for a few orbits – five to six hours. Once given the go-ahead, we will begin fuel transfer from the refuelling rocket to the shuttle bay storage tanks, and once our orbit is aligned, we will fire up the rockets and commence the TLI manoeuvre. Based on fuel reserves, the guys at NASA are working out whether or not we can get there any quicker, just in case any of the Chinese astronauts are still alive up there. So, let's mourn our loss but also, let's focus on the mission. It sounds tacky, but this is what Darryl would have wanted. Are there any questions?"

Mission specialist Jamie Harting asked the only question in her cockney accent "Do we have any idea how long their astronauts can survive on the surface?"

Hoey replied. "I was involved in assessing our information on the Chinese lunar programme. As you know, they are masters of secrecy and diversion. However, we believe they based their rocket on the Apollo configuration. That is a three-stage rocket with an orbiter and a lander. However, we assessed their rocket to be somewhat larger and able to accommodate four, maybe even five, astronauts. In Apollo, we left one person in orbit, and two went to the surface – a dangerous option as should one person gets incapacitated on the surface, the loss of the entire mission was more likely. But don't forget back then, we were in a race with the Soviets to get to the Moon first, so we scrimped. Not only that, but we got all the components built by the lowest bidder – go figure. I'm digressing. Regarding resources, Apollo 17 spent over three days on the lunar surface and could have accommodated five days easily. I would expect that for this mission, the Chinese would have included as much life support as possible, but finite nevertheless, so the sooner we get to the Moon, the more chance we have of finding anyone alive. How we can rescue any survivors is another matter entirely."

Jamie nodded, and Lance continued, "OK, let's reflect for an hour or so – then let's get back to work."

Lance, Rod and Laura stayed on the flight deck, and the other three went to the mid-deck. In such a cramped environment, it wasn't easy to get some privacy, but each did their best not to intrude on their colleagues. Laura looked through the window to the cargo bay. She could make out a portion of the silver-gold Mylar sheet that covered her friend's body. She wept some more.

# Chapter Twenty-Eight

Ran sat at his desk wearing a scowl that betrayed his dismay about the disaster that had unfolded over the past several hours. He did not lament the loss of the brave taikonauts – instead, he grieved over his loss of promotion and fame. With the management of the clandestine lunar programme and the launch's success, Ran was a shoo-in to be elected as a member of the Politburo Standing Committee of the Communist Party – a group of just nine who have extensive powers over the running of the country and its nearly 1.4 billion inhabitants. Now all his plans had turned to shit. His career was over, and he knew it. He took a large swig of Johnny Walker XR whisky. The expensive fluid was smooth and warmed his oesophagus as it went down. It was too smooth for him in his current mindset. He wished he had a cheap whisky at hand. He needed the burning of a harsh, raw drink to punish him. He looked at the report in front of him. His eyesight blurred from the alcohol, he forced himself to read it once more.

It had all started so well. The launch went to perfection, and the rocket thrusted out of the atmosphere and towards the Moon. All three stages of the rocket ignited as planned, and the taikonauts effortlessly guided the command module to extract the landing craft from the tip of the third-stage booster assembly. From there, the three-day trip to the Moon went without a hitch. The mood of all three taikonauts was high as they entered the landing craft, detached from the command module, and made their way to the surface. Without assistance from the taikonauts, they descended to the lunar surface with the aid of stereo cameras, lidar and radar tracking. Ran recalled with pride the cheers from Mission Control and the taikonauts as the contact light switched on and the lander's rocket cut out. Three of his countrymen had left Earth's confines and successfully traversed the 400,000 kilometres of the void to land safely on another world. Although the mission was to be secret for now, the Politburo would eventually acknowledge his success, and his place in history was assured. Or so he had thought. He took another swig of whisky – he felt numb, but not numb enough. Ran continued to read the report. The three taikonauts had suited up and embossed their footprints on the lunar surface. This historic moment was securely transmitted back to Beijing in full high-definition glory. He remembered the shivers which rippled along his spine as the footage of them planting the national flag was received. Tears of patriotism welled in his eyes as he wallowed in their achievement. He felt as if he was on the surface with them. He had bathed in the warmth of their collective glory.

Ran swigged back the last of his whisky, went to the credenza and grabbed another bottle. Pulling the cork, he drank directly from the bottle and returned to his desk. With diminished coordination, he brought up footage showing the taikonauts as they deployed the lunar rover and started their journey towards the structure. They had landed a couple of kilometres away from it so as not to be considered a threat should the structure have any defences. He could hear the chatter between them. They were all cheerful and excited about what they were about to encounter. Each man carried a helmet-mounted video camera that relayed footage back to the lander, where it was encrypted and forwarded to Earth. Ran used the up and down cursors, and the main image flicked between the time-synchronised taikonaut cameras and the camera mounted on the front of the rover itself. The video appeared monochromatic, with the only signs of colour coming from the red and yellow flags embossed on the taikonauts' chests, arms and helmets. Their cameras bounced around too much – Ran felt sick. He flicked to the rover feed and watched as they approached the outer perimeter of the structure. It was like a large version of Stonehenge, except that the standing stones were much more prominent and not roughly hewn. They were perfect structures with smooth flat sides and sharp ninety-degree edges. Furthermore, the capstones were part of the uprights, not separate pieces. Ran tried to gauge the distance to the structure, but there were no visual cues. As the taikonauts kangaroo-hopped towards it, the true scale of the structure became apparent. The uprights were at least 30 metres tall – around ten times the height of the stones at Stonehenge. The voice chatter between the explorers betrayed their excitement. The commander tried to be as calm as possible and relayed as much descriptive information back to Earth as possible. Finally, the taikonauts arrived at one of the uprights, and the commander reached out and touched it with his gloved hand. Although he had little tactile sensation, he could appreciate how smooth the stone was – it felt as smooth as glass. He reported that he thought this odd as the upright appeared to have a matt finish. He would have expected such a smooth object to be shiny and produce specular reflections. He unclipped a portable X-Ray fluorescence analyser from his belt and pointed it at the upright. A few seconds later, the instrument displayed information on the upright's chemical and mineralogical makeup, which he relayed to Earth. Ran paused the video and looked at a piece of paper that showed the results and annotations made by geologists and scientists at the space centre. The upright comprised regular lunar basalt – a rock similar to its Earthbound counterpart except for its higher iron content.

Ran went back to watching the commander's video feed, who expertly panned his camera over the structure – it had no seams or tool marks – it was an enigma. It was made from lunar basalt and had a highly polished surface, yet it did not have a mirrored finish. Ran watched as the commander removed a geo-pick from his belt and chipped a corner from the structure. A fist-size chunk came away with the second hit. Ran had almost expected the upright to be indestructible, akin to the monolith in Arthur C. Clarke's epic tale. The chunk missing from the upright was the only imperfection on its surface. Ran listened to the taikonauts talking about the corners' sharpness and the structure's perfection. Even a few millennia of intense solar radiation should have caused its edges to be dull, yet it hadn't. The taikonauts passed all kinds of instruments over the upright, including thermal scanners, ultraviolet light, radiometers, magnetometers and magnetic susceptibility meters. Like the XRF data, they relayed the results to the Chinese ground station in a highly compressed and encrypted form. With another swig of whisky, Ran looked at the notes associated with these readings –

nothing out of the ordinary – just lunar basalt. His attention went back to the screen as he heard the exclamation from one of the taikonauts. He had tried to place the fragment of rock back into the upright so he could measure the sample's orientation. However, the piece would not fit. Too slow for the human eye to appreciate, the upright was in the process of repairing itself. The broken part appeared inert, but the chunk missing from the upright was noticeably smaller after just 10 minutes. One of the taikonauts estimated that the structure would, for a better word, heal within a couple of hours. The taikonauts immediately started talking about nanotechnology and the possibility that miniature robots were keeping the structure in perfect condition. Using a hand-held camera, they tried to get a decent macro image of the upright but could not make out anything of significance.

Ran recalled his conversations with his scientific team once the subject of nanotechnology had arisen. Had the taikonauts become contaminated? Could they return to Earth safely, or could they represent a danger to humanity? What could they learn from the nano-bots – if they did exist? They had decided to leave these questions for later and focus on the mission. It all seemed so moot now that the taikonauts were lost, probably dead already, and the mission marked as an overwhelming disaster.

Ran fast-forwarded through the footage and watched as the three skipped towards the centre of the structure. The ground they hopped over looked like typical lunar regolith, with craters of all sizes scattered around the place and superimposed on one another. As they moved, lunar dust made neat parabolas in front of them. With no atmosphere to intervene, the dust did not bellow – nothing remained suspended in the sky. As they approached the centre of the structure, they came across a featureless black rectangle on the ground. At first, it looked to be a shaft, but as they got closer, it was clear that they were approaching a ramp that descended deep into the regolith. The taikonauts stood at the ramp's edge and took a similar set of measurements as for the upright. One taikonaut knelt and measured the slope of the ramp – it was precisely 30 degrees to the horizontal. Ran watched as the taikonauts switched on their suit lights and saw the perfectly flat walls and floor as the commander descended into the structure.

Without warning, the commander's feed went black. Ran switched to the time-synchronised video feed of the pilot. When the commander's video feed died, the pilot could still see the commander several paces ahead. Then, without warning, the pilot's video feed also went dead. Ran switched to the co-pilot's feed and watched in amazement as he tried to enter deeper into the tunnel. However, something prevented him from moving forward – he was restricted by some invisible force. He could make out the other two taikonauts through the co-pilot's suit camera as they returned to their comrade. However, they were just as stuck on the other side of the invisible barrier. The co-pilot could not use his radio to communicate with the other two taikonauts. In a panic, he tried to communicate via gesticulation, but doing so in a pressurised space suit proved to be a fruitless exercise. Ran listened to the co-pilot's conversation with Mission Control, who ordered him to use explosives to break through the barrier. The co-pilot removed a charge pack from his kit and placed it on the floor at the base of the invisible wall. His two comrades saw this and immediately retreated deep into the tunnel – well outside the co-pilot's field of view. The charge was directional – essentially the Chinese equivalent of a claymore mine and comprised several dozen ball bearings encased within plastic explosives. He unwound a cable from the device and retreated several metres. He lifted a missile switch cover on a small box, crouched down the best he could and pressed the button. A bright and silent flash lit the environment, but there was no sound or pressure wave. The taikonaut returned to the barrier and was amazed at what he saw. The ball bearings were suspended in space in a perfect plane, falling slowly to the ground – much slower than one would expect even under the Moon's one-sixth of Earth's gravity. He waited for his two comrades to re-appear, but they didn't. He tried to enter the ramp but could not. Panic again set in, greater this time, and it took Mission Control several minutes to calm him down. Finally, they ordered him to make his way back to the lunar module and await further instructions. Ran knew the rest and switched off the feed. His scowl unabated, he took another swig of whisky, wiped his mouth on his immaculate, tailored French-cuffed business shirt, buried his head in his hands, and cried in selfish self-pity.

The crew of Discovery had just finished sending personal messages of condolences to the family of Darryl Candy. Laura, Jamie and Kurt bobbed around in the mid-deck compartment supping on drink packs.

"I guess Darryl is number 15 on NASA's wall," Jamie spoke first.

"18," Kurt replied with a sigh.

"What do you mean? Seven died on Challenger and another seven on Columbia. That makes Darryl the 15th," Jamie responded.

"You forget the Apollo 1 fire. Grissom, White, and Chaffee died in the capsule. They were officially on a mission and, although they did not leave the ground, they are considered the US's first astronauts lost in the line of duty."

"15, 18... we see them as numbers now and not as people," Kurt said.

During this time, Laura, who had been daydreaming, was thinking of Darryl Candy and the fun they shared during astronaut training as the only two rookies on the mission. She snapped back to the present when she heard Kurt say 1518. "What's important about 1518?" Laura asked.

"You must have been miles away, Laura. We weren't talking about a year, but the number of astronauts lost on American missions. We've lost 15 in flight and three on the ground." Kurt explained.

Laura gave a vacant nod in acknowledgement and drifted towards her tablet computer. The number 1518 was in the notes of Richard Fairbrother. She thought the number referred to the year 1518 and remembered trying to determine the significance of that year. There had been a transit of Venus – and there was one this year as well – and there won't be another until 2117. The only major event recorded in the history books for 1518 was the so-called dance plague in Strasbourg, France. It was a strange epidemic that caused the afflicted to start dancing uncontrollably. The cause remains a mystery, with some saying that bread tainted with ergot fungus essentially drugged many of the population with a natural form of LSD. Others believe it was the result of shared stress-induced psychosis. Over a month, some 400 people were affected, and several dozen died from dehydration, heart attacks or strokes due to the uncontrollable urge to dance.

Her fingers swiped across the screen. None of the other astronauts had been made aware of Project Star Gate and the notes and recordings of the Richard and Peter Fairbrother. It took a few seconds to find the page. It contained the number 1518, a lightning bolt and what appeared to be a walking stick. Although Laura would never understand the true significance of the lightning bolt – it identified a bolt in a Molniya orbit as the cause – it eventually clicked that the walking stick could be a Christmas candy cane – a reference to Darryl Candy. If only she had worked this out without hindsight, Darryl might still be alive.

She shook her head and tried to figure out the paradoxes of the Fairbrothers. It made her head spin. How could they see what they saw? If Leo had never found the notes of Richard Fairbrother, she would not have to process the LRO data, and she wouldn't be orbiting Earth in a space shuttle rescued from retirement. The only conclusion she could make was that free will was an illusion that did not exist. Somehow, the future was fixed according to a reality in which effect is predetermined, regardless of cause. Humanity was following some kind of playbook, which did not sit well with Laura.

Rod Hoey poked his head through the mid-deck and flight deck portal. "OK, guys, time to focus on the mission. We've just completed the fuel transfer to our shuttle-bay tanks, and we need to get ready for trans-lunar injection. Could you please configure your seats, stow any loose objects and get ready for some acceleration? We are waiting to hear from Mission Control but are looking at a go-no-go for TLI in around 40 minutes or so."

The status update generated some excitement with the rest of the crew. It was going to happen – they were off to the Moon!

# Chapter Thirty

Laura sat strapped into the same chair as for launch. This time she wore just her blue coveralls –much more comfortable than the pumpkin suit. She looked to her right and lamented the absence of Darryl Candy. His chair remained stowed – none of the other crew wanted to take his seat on the primary flight deck.

She overheard Rod Hoey talking to Mission Control and watched as he typed commands into the shuttle's now aging and technically obsolete flight computer. Lance verified each command as it was entered and repeated the words along with the customary 'check' at the end of each sentence. With a final button press, the crew felt a rumble and gentle build-up of pressure as all three main engines on Discovery and the three on the rocket booster ignited to plan.

"All lights green Mission Control, fuel rate within parameters, navigation all good, over." Rod relayed to Houston in his typical ice-cool tone. Based on n-body and patched conics, NASA had calculated an optimal trajectory to get them to the Moon more quicker. The shuttle was presently accelerating away from the Moon, instead following a path that would bring Discovery to apogee close to the radius of the Moon's orbit. They timed the burn so that the Moon would be close to the shuttle at the time of apogee. Discovery will then alter its orbit hyperbolically to enter its sphere of influence and become a satellite of Earth's only natural satellite.

A little over eight minutes had passed when the main engines powered down smoothly, and the crew felt a clunk as the umbilicals disconnected and the brackets unlocked. Small thrusters pushed the exhausted refuelling rocket away from Discovery. Laura felt the mild discomfort of a return to weightlessness. Rod Hoey was in touch with Mission Control. He removed his harness and positioned himself so that everyone could hear him.

"Good news, guys; we've had a successful trans-lunar injection burn, and the next stop is the Moon!" The excitement in Rod's voice broke through his normally calm tones. Cheers, claps and whoops of joy echoed throughout the cabin.

Laura floated around the flight deck, diverting her attention from the view of Earth from the shuttle-bay window to the growing Moon visible from the pilot's side window. Earth appeared much smaller now – the Moon seemed much more prominent than she was accustomed to, and it looked more three-dimensional than it ever appeared from Earth. She made herself comfortable and began reviewing the notes Peter Fairbrother had made for her. These had been transcribed and stored on her touchpad computer. Laura was aware that Peter Fairbrother received his 'communications' verbally, unlike his father, who had experienced visions. However, whether this made Peter Fairbrother's notes any more legible was a matter of debate. Many of the messages were very cryptic – perhaps this was for the best. He recalled what Peter had said to her – that she was the 'chosen one'. What did that mean? Peter had told her she would meet with the Gods and become an angel. Does that mean she will die? What purpose would that serve in the grand scheme of things? She flicked over more of his notes: 'stand in the centre' – 'red is a colour not to fear' – 'don't fight the tingling; it will only make things worse.' There was a multitude of such snippets, many of which sounded almost Confucian, but none made any real sense to Laura.

A flash distracted Laura for a second. So far, she had experienced a few of these and had found them annoying. First reported by the Apollo 11 astronauts, these flashes were high-energy cosmic rays passing through her head and exciting neurons in her visual cortex. Such rays were rare on Earth, having been stopped by its strong magnetic field.

Laura returned attention to her touchpad and came across a page where the same sentence was repeated over and over again: 'You will make a choice that affects all of humanity.' It put chills up her spine.

Lance Halas popped his head through the hatch and asked Laura to join the rest of the crew in the mid-deck compartment. Earlier that day, he had received a transmission from the GSFC that he wanted everyone to see.

"We received some information about the Chinese situation a few hours ago. The GSFC re-tasked the Lunar Reconnaissance Orbiter and passed us some good images of what they have been doing on the surface. The imagery is incomplete, but I'm afraid things don't look too good for them." Halas reported. He passed around his tablet computer and showed a series of images obtained from the LRO. The first showed the landing site, where many footprints and disturbed regolith and it was possible to make out the Chinese flag. The second picture showed their rover several hundred metres from the structure's perimeter. Between the rover and the structure were four sets of footprints.

"They've got four astronauts down there?" exo-biologist Brian Paris asked.

"That's what the GSFC thought at first." Halas replied, "If you look closer to the bottom, you will see a single set of prints heading towards their lander, between the rover's tracks. It looks as if three astronauts headed to the structure, but only one returned, leaving the rover where it was and heading back to the lander on foot."

"So, there's a chance that at least one of the astronauts is alive and holed up in the lander?" Laura asked.

"That's what the GSFC and NASA believe. Due to the extremely low altitude of the LRO and the field of view of the camera, we cannot get full coverage of the area for several days. The LRO is low on fuel, and there needs to be a critical reason to change its orbit again." Halas said.

Laura wondered what the Chinese astronauts had encountered. Why had two people stayed in the structure? Why had only one returned to the lander? She felt uneasy – a feeling of foreboding washed over her.

A little under four days had passed since launch, and Discovery was about to enter lunar orbit. Rod Hoey and Lance Halas were at their controls, going through a checklist and relaying information back to Earth. The delay in round-trip communications had already become apparent. They were nearly 1.3 light seconds away from Houston, taking over 2.5 seconds for round-trip communications. It forced everyone to speak slowly and clearly and to terminate their message with the word 'over'.

The rest of the crew had made their way onto the flight deck, and Halas informed them to expect gentle g-forces as they manoeuvred Discovery into a stable lunar orbit. Rod Hoey entered commands into the flight computer, which Halas checked, and pressed the execute button. A few seconds passed before the hiss of positioning thrusters could be heard. The stars appeared to move as Discovery turned around. A few minutes later, they felt the gradual build-up of the shuttle's main engines, taking the orbiter out of its hyperbolic geocentric trajectory and into a circular selenocentric one. Hoey and Halas conferred with Houston, during which time Hoey made a few manual burns. They then received confirmation from Houston that they had successfully entered lunar orbit. Halas flicked the intercom button so the crew could hear the clapping from Mission Control. There were smiles all around as those on Discovery clapped, shook hands and 'high-fived' one another.

Once the excitement died down, Halas addressed the crew. "We've made it, guys, but we are here on a mission, and we must all be on the ball – even more so given the loss of Darryl. I want the landing party to have a sleep period of around six hours. Consider it an order to take a pill if you are too excited to sleep. Remember that we will spend quite some time in our EVA suits – maybe a day or two – so get prepared for the mental and physical implications of this. Rod and Jamie, you will have the pleasure of each other's company for a while. As discussed, we will use Darryl's position on the moonhopper to transport his body to the surface and potentially bring a Chinese survivor back to Discovery."

Rod grinned, but it had a twinge of sadness to it. After all, he had just travelled the nearly 400,000km between Earth and the Moon, yet like Mike Collins of Apollo 11, his footprints will never adorn the lunar regolith.

"I'll have plenty to keep me busy up here, Lance," Hoey commented.

"OK, six hours in the sack, an hour to eat, shit and shave, and a couple of hours getting suited up and pre-breathed. From there, we are looking at about an hour to deploy the hopper and ease that baby onto the surface. So, in 12 hours, we expect to have four more pairs of American feet on the Moon, as well as the body of our friend and colleague Darryl Candy. Snap to it." Lance ordered without a trace of a smile.

All members of the landing party took a pill to help them sleep. In truth, Hoey was somewhat depressed in that he was so close yet far from the Moon. If Jamie was disappointed, she didn't show it. The payload and mission specialists each took one of the four rigid sleeping compartments on the mid-deck whilst Halas and Hoey slid into sleeping bags attached to the forward storage lockers. They donned eye masks and drifted to sleep in the womb-like comfort of zero-g.

# Chapter Thirty-Three

With the aid of pharmaceuticals, all members of the landing party awoke to the sound of the alarm clock, feeling refreshed and alert. Together they shared a high-protein breakfast and chatted about what they would likely encounter on the surface. Then one by one, they made the best use of the shuttle's toilet facility and stepped into the much-hated diapers that would hold their waste, possibly for a day or two. Laura had always romanticised the role of an astronaut. However, thinking of hopping around on the Moon wearing a wet, or worse, soiled diaper instantly destroyed that thought.

Donned in a diaper and long johns, Laura thought she looked like some hick from a trailer-trash park – except her clothes were too clean. She slipped into a fresh blue jumpsuit and felt somewhat more professional. From there, she guided herself into the airlock, where she met Kurt, who was already sealed inside his Constellation class EVA suit. Laura's suit was there also, and Kurt motioned for her to hop into it. Together they went through the process of checking each suit's seal integrity and began their pre-breathing exercises. Laura swivelled around to see Halas and Paris getting into their spacesuits. Her heart rate increased when she saw Rod move over and close the inner hatch of the airlock.

"It's a walk in the park… it's a walk in the park," Laura mumbled as Kurt opened the outer hatch. She breathed in until she could breathe no more. She thought she was choking until she realised she just needed to exhale.

"Not quite a walk in the park." Kurt replied with a snigger, "Don't forget we are on a continuous open mic."

Laura hoped that her transmission hadn't made it to Houston. Kurt, now outside of the airlock, motioned for Laura's hand. She grabbed it, and he guided her out of the airlock and into the open shuttle bay. Laura gasped as she saw that the moonhopper had already been taken out of storage using the shuttle's manipulator arm and was standing proud of the shuttle bay. Rod and Jamie had awoken earlier and had expertly extracted the strange contraption from the cargo bay while the landing party slept. Strange was an appropriate word to describe the moonhopper. It had five spindly carbon fibre landing legs that protruded three metres from a large rocket pack. Above that was a pentagonal column, about two metres in diameter, with a hatch on each facet. Laura couldn't believe that Brad had devised the idea for such a creation.

"Hold on here," Kurt asked Laura. "I need to seal the airlock hatch so the others can join us."

It was the most frightening yet exhilarating moment of her life. Laura looked up to see the Moon taking up her entire field of vision. If she reached out, she thought it would be possible to touch its surface. Bathed in the Sun's light reflected off the lunar surface, colours seemed different to Laura. Whites seemed more steely-white than the warm white experienced on Earth, and blues seemed much more vibrant. Together and without any form of harness, and using only their arms, Kurt and Laura shimmied up the shuttle's manipulator arm and towards the moonhopper. Kurt asked Laura to stay put at the point where the manipulator arm and moonhopper connected. Expertly, Kurt flipped around and commenced an inspection of the craft. He went to a control panel and proceeded to power up its systems. Happy that everything was in order, Kurt made his way back to Laura and helped her connect the backpack of her Constellation suit to one of the hatches of the moonhopper.

"Laura, you OK?" Kurt asked. "I have to go and retrieve Darryl's body and strap him into the place beside you."

"I'm OK, Kurt – I just wish Darryl was still with us to share in this amazing experience," Laura replied.

Kurt nodded and shimmied down the manipulator arm and back into the shuttle bay. A few minutes passed that to Laura felt like hours. She realised she was literally plugged into an unproven vehicle suspended upside down several kilometres above the lunar surface.

Could reality get any more absurd, she thought as she stared up, or was it down, at the Moon, watching the highlands, basalt seas, and a myriad of craters pass by.

Laura glimpsed the body of Darryl Candy out of the corner of her eye. Kurt had secured the silver-gold Mylar blanket around Darryl's helmet and opted to ascend the manipulator arm from the other side to not distress Laura. Kurt used simple nylon webbing to strap the body onto the moonhopper. Laura could hear Kurt sniffing over the open mic – he had been crying as he performed the macabre task.

Kurt waited at the top of the manipulator arm for Brian Paris and Lance Halas to arrive. He ensured everyone was securely attached to the moonhopper and extended the pilot control arms that allowed Halas to control the moonhopper and manually pilot it should the need arise. Finally satisfied that everybody was secure, Kurt positioned himself and, using two handholds, pushed himself into the moonhopper's remaining hatch until he felt a satisfying click. From his side, he pulled out an arm that contained a series of controls. Activating the head-up display in his suit, Kurt waited a couple of seconds for the establishment of a wireless connection between his spacesuit and the moonhopper. Kurt went through a systems checklist projected onto his visor using a contraption similar to an oversized gamer's mouse. He relayed his satisfaction to Halas, who then activated his head-up display. Happy that everything was running to spec, he contacted Hoey to disengage the moonhopper from the manipulator arm. Hoey gave the arm a gentle push before he opened the grabber and the moonhopper floated slowly away from the shuttle. When it was about 50m from Discovery, Halas entered the first of the pre-programmed commands and jets all over the craft fired independently of one another. The moonhopper rotated so that its spindly legs pointed towards the lunar surface. Downward pointing cameras mapped the surface of the Moon, and this, in conjunction with laser altimeters and old-fashioned inertial guidance systems, allowed the moonhopper to ascertain its exact position.

"Discovery, this is Grissom. We have a locational lock, and our guidance is good… repeat guidance is good, over." Halas radioed back to Discovery, who relayed the message back to Houston.

A reply from Rod Hoey came a few seconds later. "Grissom, Discovery, you have a go; repeat, you have a go for landing. Godspeed, over."

"Roger that, over and out," Lance responded, tapping a button on his control pad. Descent plans appeared on his visor, along with projected fuel use. The descent plan had them landing within 300 metres of the Chinese lander. If someone had survived, they would likely be using the last of the lander's life support. At the very least, they could offer some additional reserves – perhaps even deploy an emergency shelter. Once Darryl Candy had been laid to rest, there was a spot for a taikonaut on the moonhopper. Should the other two taikonauts still be alive, it was possible to take them back to the shuttle in the central column or via multiple trips.

Lance heard a pinging noise in his helmet, indicating that a manoeuvre was about to commence. He felt the various thrusters fire as the whole craft tilted about sixty degrees from vertical. The main engine then pulsed: it was the main de-orbit burn. The moonhopper started to fall into the Moon's weak gravitational well.

Laura and the other astronauts experienced conflicting emotions of terror and exhilaration. They had nothing to do but wait and watch as their amusement park ride took them to their destination.

Throughout the descent, stereo cameras, laser and radar systems mapped out the terrain in three dimensions with millimetre accuracy. In the distance, Halas could make out the shape of the Chinese lander and then realised that they had just passed over the tracks scored into the thin regolith by their rover. However, he couldn't make out any footprints. Halas checked the altitude – around 50 metres. If the taikonaut had followed the rover tracks back to the lander, they hadn't made it back.

More pinging noises filled Halas' helmet: it was the proximity notification warning. Like a car's reversing sensor, the pings sounded faster until they merged into a single coherent tone. One last snap of thrust from the main engine and the high-tensile carbon-fibre legs of the lander dug into the surface of the Moon. The energy built up during landing transferred back through these, and the whole craft hopped almost a metre before settling to rest.

"Houston, Grissom has landed… Repeat Grissom has landed." Lance felt relieved that the moonhopper had passed its first and probably most dangerous part of the mission without a single hiccup.

A few seconds later came congratulations from Rod Hoey and a report from Houston a minute after that.

"Grissom, Houston. We follow you down, and the whole of Mission Control, as well as the Whitehouse, wish to congratulate you all on the successful return of the US to the Moon after an absence of almost 40 years. Grissom, you have permission to inspect the Chinese lander for survivors and to pay our last respects to Darryl Candy. By the way, I have just heard that Darryl has been awarded the Presidential Medal of Freedom, the highest award our country can bestow on a civilian. Over and out."

Halas addressed the astronauts, "OK, guys, you've heard the news from Houston. We've just made history. We've got a couple of things to do here. First, I think we all want to place a footprint or two on the surface. We need to check the Chinese lander for survivors, but I didn't see any footprints coming this way, so I don't expect to find anyone home. We need to lay Darryl to rest, and, as is customary, we need to plant a flag. You've all done the training, so please lean back while Kurt disengages you from the moonhopper. Keep your wits about you, and let's be safe."

# Chapter Thirty-Four
Lunar Surface T+4d:3h:11m

Each astronaut felt their suit disengage from the moonhopper. Halas turned around and descended a spidery ladder built into the lander's legs. Without words or ceremony, he hopped off the disk at the end of the leg and onto the lunar surface. However, high resolutions cameras within the lander captured the moment. Equipment in the lander broadcasted the footage to Discovery and on to Houston in a continual invisible encrypted stream of zeros and ones.

Halas made his way around the other side of the moonhopper. Kurt was on the platform using a jury-rigged block and tackle to lower Darryl Candy's corpse to the ground. Halas took the weight as they lowered the body and gently laid it on the ground in the shadow of the moonhopper.

He then hopped around to each leg of the lander and assisted each astronaut as they made their way down the ladder.

"We're here. We are actually here!" Laura said in exasperation.

"I think you're going to have to pinch me. It doesn't feel real." Exo-biologist Brian Paris replied.

"Well, we are here, and we have a job to do. Before we check out the Chinese lander, I will look at the rover tracks. As we were coming in, I couldn't make out any footprints heading back this way. Not a good sign." Halas said, and without waiting for a reply, he skipped toward the departure point of the rover.

The other astronauts were eyes agog and were drinking in their surroundings. Buzz Aldrin had coined the phrase 'magnificent desolation,' and Laura considered he was right on the money. There was so little on the Moon's surface, yet Laura, Kurt and Brian appeared to be suffering from sensory overload. Before they knew it, Halas had re-joined the group.

"It's as I expected. No footprints are heading back in this direction. It doesn't look like the taikonaut made his way back to the lander. But let's take a quick look if they have a fourth astronaut in their team and relay our findings back to Houston." Halas said.

Having the same mass but under the influence of only one-sixth of Earth's gravity and wearing a considerable amount of equipment makes walking on the Moon a rather strange and unique experience. The first men on the Moon, Neil Armstrong and Edwin "Buzz" Aldrin, had quickly determined that a sideways skip was one of the easiest and least stressful ways to move around. It was too easy to miscalculate one's momentum when moving forward with the result of landing on your belly. However, by skipping at an angle, you had the benefit of steadying yourself with a partly extended leg on each hop.

Like children playing horsey, Laura and the other three astronauts skipped towards the Chinese lander. Laura couldn't help but think of the Monty Python movie Brad had introduced to her. If only she had a couple of coconut halves to clap together – not that you would hear them in the vacuum of space.

After a few minutes of hopping and they reached the Chinese lander. As Mission Commander, Halas approached the craft and began climbing the cockpit ladder. The door was unlocked and ajar. He swung the door open and peered inside. Automatically the lights on his helmet activated, and its attached camera continued to capture high-resolution images of everything Halas saw. Although there were some differences, mainly in size, the layout bore a remarkable similarity to the Apollo lunar landers of forty years earlier. Why invent when you can copy, Halas thought.

Without completely entering the capsule, Lance hopped down the ladder and radioed a report to Houston. He relayed to Mission Control that the Chinese lander had only three seats, with no signs that any crew had returned. In the time it took for him to make the report, Mission Control had received the images from his helmet camera and was in the process of enhancing them for future analysis.

Over the next twenty minutes, the four astronauts gathered around the body of Darryl Candy. Covered with a Mylar sheet tacked down by a few rocks and draped in the flag of the USA, Lance gave a simple yet elegant Eulogy. Laura, Kurt and Brian each provided a few words about the person they had trained with for over a year and who had become as close as a brother to them.

The four then went through a flag-raising ceremony to mark their landing. Without an atmosphere, a carbon fibre rod allowed the flag to stand proudly on the surface. A few inches from the flag, Laura knelt and grabbed a handful of Moon dust and a few centimetre-sized rocks that she poured into a small snap-lock bag, sealed it and placed it into a pocket on the right leg of her suit.

They made their way back to the moonhopper and climbed back onto the platform. The weak lunar gravity made connecting their backpacks to the moonhopper much easier; within five minutes, all were ready to proceed. Lance tapped in commands that would take the moonhopper in a direction parallel to the Chinese rover towards the feature. The commands would also keep the moonhopper closer to the surface rather than the larger sweeping arcs it was designed to do. This would result in a higher fuel burn rate, but they would see more of the surface as they travelled to the structure.

He pressed the execute button, and the main engine fired, followed by bursts from two lateral thrusters. The moonhopper rose in an arc around 50 metres high and, with the impulse imparted by the lateral thrusters, moved around 400 metres before the engines cut back in, and the craft made another gentle landing. Another hop of a similar distance and the moonhopper landed within 50 metres of the Chinese rover. From the few metres of elevation afforded by the moonhopper, Halas traced the footprints from the rover heading towards the Chinese lander. About 100 metres away from the rover, he could make out the crumpled pile that was one of the Chinese taikonauts. Halas programmed in a short deviation hop and expertly directed the moonhopper to within 10 metres of the astronaut. He disengaged from the lander and made their way on foot to the body with Kurt. As they had expected, the astronaut was dead; his oxygen stocks were depleted. They didn't realise that a ball bearing from the explosive charge had ricocheted off the barrier and grazed the taikonaut's suit. The leak had been small but consistent and was in a place where the hands could not reach to repair it. Halas managed to kneel and say a silent prayer.

Back on the moonhopper, they made a short jump to the Chinese rover. As they inspected it, they all came to the same conclusion; one that defied all logic. It appeared that the taikonaut had tried to hotwire the rover, which had an ignition key.

"What moron would put a key on a lunar rover?" Halas questioned.

"Damned if I know, Lance. I know the Chinese are a naturally suspicious mob, but I don't know who they thought would want to steal their rover up here." Kurt replied.

Lance got close to the rover to ensure they got as many useful photos as possible. Shaking his head in disbelief, Lance instructed Kurt it was time to go, and they made their way back to the moonhopper. Lance reprogrammed the flight plan for the most economical trajectories and entered a landing location 50 metres from the boundary of the structure.

"All aboard... Next stop, alien structure." Brian Paris said in a poorly imitated British accent.

Not too impressed with the silliness, Halas said nothing and pressed the command button. The moonhopper bounded into space in a wide parabola. Lance and Kurt had good views of the alien structure and gasped when they saw the sheer size of it. On the other hand, Laura and Brian had to make do with a video feed projected onto their visors.

Another series of precisely delivered bursts of thrust, and the spindly contraption came to a gentle halt. They all disengaged from the moonhopper and made their way down their ladders. Everyone was in awe when they saw the structure first-hand – it was large and precisely constructed. Kurt used a laser range finder to measure the exact distance to the feature. This information, along with the focal length of his stereo high-resolution helmet camera, allowed Mission Control to measure the structure's dimensions.

They made their way to the structure. Kurt recorded signs of radiation, whether it be radiogenic, electromagnetic or magnetic in nature, but noted nothing out of the ordinary.

When they reached one of the uprights, they used a portable XRF unit to discover that the structure comprised regular lunar basalt.

Brian Paris was the first to mention the incongruence, "The surface feels polished… If this is lunar basalt, it should be shiny, but it's not. Can I chip off a sample for analysis?"

Lance thought about it. "Let's grab a sample on the way back. I don't think it will reflect well if we smash up the place and bump into the little green occupants."

Under Lance's command, they proceeded to the centre of the structure, following the four sets of Chinese footprints – three that led towards the centre and one that led away.

"I wish we had some weapons," Brian mentioned.

"If there are still aliens here, I don't think any weapon we have will be much of a match for them," Kurt replied.

"Forget the aliens – I'm talking about the Chinese!" Brian responded.

That thought had also crossed Lance's mind, but the no-weapons directive had come directly from the top. Little did he know that this directive was based on Leo Helfgott's interpretation of Richard Fairbrother's notes.

About fifteen metres from the central ramp, Kurt deployed a small communications relay station: a battery and solar-powered device relaying to Discovery signals sent to it via optic fibre. Kurt switched the device on and conducted a system check with Rod Hoey aboard the shuttle to ensure it worked to spec. Kurt clipped the fibre optic cable reel to his belt and was careful it was deployed without any damage as they made their way towards the ramp.

Lance was the first to see the long length of wire attached to a small box on the ground. With some difficulty, he knelt on one knee and picked up the box to examine it.

"What is it?" Kurt asked.

"I can't read the Chinese characters, but it looks like a trigger switch for an explosive to me. Did you read that Discovery?" Lance said.

"Roger that, Lance. I will notify Houston. Take care down there, over and out." Rod replied.

They followed the trigger cable to its end – it terminated cleanly at where the ramp started. It didn't look right to Lance. He had some experience laying charges as part of his military past, and usually, trigger cables show more damage. Perhaps it was the lack of atmosphere on the Moon, Lance concluded. He looked around – there was no sign of any divot in the regolith and no other evidence they had used an explosive device. The entrance to the ramp was around five metres across, and the walls were as smooth as the uprights, the edges sharp and precise. The four astronauts walked onto the ramp, enabled their helmet lamps, and gingerly moved forward.

Kurt kept in radio contact with Discovery as they descended the ramp. He tried to describe his surroundings, but they were so non-descript that he reverted to asking for a radio check every few seconds.

Lance estimated they were about five metres below the surface. Nothing had changed; the walls were perfectly smooth and uniform, and they saw no other artefacts. On his next step, however, Lance noticed an environmental change.

"Did you guys notice that?" Lance asked.

"Notice what?" Laura replied as she took her next step, "Oh, I see what you mean."

All four astronauts noticed that it took an additional effort to take a step forward. They all looked down to see if the pitch of the ramp had changed – it hadn't.

Lance's next step took even more effort, and his third even more. Expecting the fourth to require even more, he was surprised when it proved effortless. He was also surprised to find the tunnel flooded with light. He took a few more steps forward and turned around. His three fellow astronauts looked around the structure's interior in awe.

"Where's the light coming from?" Laura was the first to ask. "There doesn't seem to be any light sources around, yet there's ambient light."

Kurt interjected, "We've lost contact with Discovery. It may have something to do with that… 'barrier' we passed through. I request permission to go back to the last point of contact."

"Go do it, Kurt. Let them know what we have just experienced and that we will submit hourly status reports. We'll wait here for you.

We'll come looking for you if you're not back in five minutes." Lance replied.

Surprisingly, hopping up the ramp took less effort than going down. Kurt experienced the same few steps of resistance and suddenly found himself engulfed in total darkness. He switched his helmet lights back on and was doubly relieved when he heard the voice of Rod Hoey over his headset. Kurt explained the lack of communication within the tunnel, the zone of resistance and the strange lighting. They agreed to the regular status reports. Kurt then tried to contact the other astronauts but could not. Eventually, he made his way back down the ramp, where he reencountered the strange resistance. Suddenly he was bathed in light and saw his fellow astronauts.

"Wow!" Laura exclaimed, "You just appeared out of nowhere."

"You noticed that too!" Brian Paris said in disbelief. "Do you think we went through some kind of transporter?"

Kurt laughed. "I think you've watched too much Star Trek, Brian. If something had transported us, my fibre optic cable would have severed. I had no problems getting back into signal range with Discovery, and they expect hourly reports from us."

"OK, let's explore this tunnel, guys. Kurt, can you place one of the motion-sensing cameras here just in case there are still little green men around?" Lance requested.

Preconfigured, it took only a minute or two for Kurt to set up and test the camera. Sitting on a little tripod, the camera instantly picked up the movement of the astronauts and focused on their activity. Kurt tapped the control panel on his cuff, and the feed from the camera appeared on his visor display. Happy that all was in order, he unclipped the fibre optic reel from his belt, left it on the floor beside the camera, and headed off down the tunnel with the others.

They continued down the straight featureless ramp for several minutes. Kurt commented that they must be close to being directly under the 'standing stones' that mark the structure's perimeter. With some mental math, he estimated that they were around 50m below the lunar surface.

After a few more minutes of walking, they reached the tunnel's end. The floor levelled out, and they entered a large, hollow chamber that appeared to be a perfect cube, approximately 15m a side. The floors, walls and ceilings were all uniform dark grey of lunar basalt, and all were utterly featureless.

Just a few metres from the tunnel's entry, Paris made a discovery when he came across the crumpled suit of a Chinese taikonaut. Brian and Laura hopped over, and Laura peered through the visor. The bloated, lifeless face of the Chinese man stared back at her. She stumbled backwards in horror. Paris noted that the taikonaut's oxygen and power reserves were exhausted.

"This doesn't make any sense," Laura said.

"What doesn't? He ran out of oxygen and power, so he died." Brian replied.

"He shouldn't be decomposing, Brian. Without power, his temperature, especially this far under the lunar surface, should be close to that of deep space. He should be frozen." Laura replied.

Kurt overheard the conversation and checked the sensor readings on his suit. "You're right, Laura; I've just checked the environmental sensors – I didn't think to check until now – but it seems the ambient temperature in this chamber is a rather pleasant 25 degrees Celsius."

"Here! Now!" The voice of Lance Halas came over their headsets.

All three moved as fast as they could to Lance's position. Standing over the body of the second taikonaut, they saw that his visor was open and his eyes were closed. Laura stared at the face, her confusion rising.

"This isn't right," Laura said. "His face should have bloated and disfigured in a vac…"

Kurt cut in. "You didn't let me finish. The temperature is a pleasant 25 degrees Celsius, and the pressure is a little over 100 kilopascals – similar to the atmospheric pressure at sea level on Ear…"

Lance and Laura stumbled backwards, with Laura ending up on her rear, as the Chinese man's eyes opened, and he let out a blood-curdling scream.

# Chapter Thirty-Five

Lunar Facility T+4d:5h:22m

It took a while to calm the man down. Lance tapped on his shoulder to bring the taikonaut's attention to the flag of the USA. This seemed to work; he nodded, swallowed hard, and his breathing eased.

Lance accessed the control panel on his cuff and switched off his oxygen and power supply. He then opened the hatch to the back of his suit and stepped out. He took a deep breath – the air smelt like spent gunpowder, which he had expected. The Apollo astronauts experienced the same small in the cabin of the lander. Apparently, it was due to the Moon dust. However, the reason for this odour remained a mystery even after forty years.

Lance reached back into his suit, extracted his backup communicator and asked Kurt and Brian to go back and make a report of what had just transpired. He also informed them that their next contact would be in three hours. He then told Laura that it was OK to get out of her suit – which she did with a bit of assistance from Lance.

It was refreshing being out of the suit. She removed her snoopy hat, threw it into her spacesuit, and closed its hatch. She then went over to the Chinese taikonaut.

"Can you speak any English?" Laura asked the Chinese astronaut in a slow, clear voice.

"Yes, quite a bit, but please speak slowly," he replied.

Laura smiled, "My name is Laura. What is yours?" She asked.

"My name is Kong She Rui, but you can call me Gordon." He said with a wry smile.

Lance radioed the man's details to Kurt and asked him to relay the information to Houston.

"What happened?" Laura asked.

"We landed and used our rover to get here. We entered the ramp

164

and reached, what I can only call, some kind of invisible wall. I was able to pass through it along with Zhao, but Jiao could not get through. Did Jiao make it back to the lander?" Gordon replied.

Sadness filled Laura's eyes, and she shook her head. "I'm afraid not, Gordon. He returned to the rover, but I don't think he had a key. From there, he tried to make it back to the lander but didn't make it. I'm so sorry." Laura said and continued. "Do you know why he couldn't get through the barrier?"

He shook his head. "Zhao had the key to the rover. No, we had no idea why he could not get in. Furthermore, we could not get out. He even tried to set off a charge to get to us. We went deep inside the tunnel for the detonation but could not return to the exit. We were trapped. We explored the tunnel, and when we got to this chamber, we could not find any other tunnel or room. It's a dead end. We sat here conserving our oxygen, waiting for rescue, but no one came. Zhao ran out of oxygen first and died. I decided to commit suicide and opened my helmet only to discover that there was an atmosphere down here. We should have known as our suits no longer felt bloated." Gordon lamented.

Lance knelt beside Gordon and looked up a Laura. "We've had no problems crossing the barrier in either direction. Why do you think that is, Laura?"

Laura thought about it, and it clicked. "Gordon, did you or Zhao carry any weapons or explosives with you?" she asked.

"No, only Jiao had weapons – a gun and some explosive packs." He replied.

"I think carrying a weapon put this facility into some sort of lock-down and prevented travel through the barrier in either direction," Laura remarked.

Lance entered the discussion. "Gordon, my name is Lance Halas, and I am the commander of this expedition. First, we will find a way to get you safely back home. For that, we will need to work together. Do you understand?"

Gordon nodded, and a smile betrayed his relief. "Thank you." He replied.

"You look remarkably well, considering you have been here at least four days. How are you doing for food and water?" Lance asked.

"Four days… I didn't realise. I haven't eaten or drunk anything since landing. For some reason, while in this chamber, I have had no desire to eat or drink. I don't feel hungry and have no urge to toilet. Something here sustains me, and I think it has something to do with nanotechnology." Gordon replied and continued to explain their observations when they had chipped a sample from one of the uprights.

"That would explain why we didn't see any sign of the explosion at the entrance," Lance said. He glanced at his spacesuit. Where grey lunar dust once clung to his trousers, it now looked new, as if taken directly out of his storage locker on Discovery. "Look at my suit… it's clean. There's not a speck of lunar dust to be seen!"

Laura went to her suit and extracted the snap-lock bag from the pocket of her trouser leg. The sample of Moon dust and rock was intact inside the bag, but not a speck of dust was seen on the exterior.

"Well, if it is nano-tech, there is quite a bit of intelligence behind it," Laura remarked and placed the sample bag back into the pocket.

Lance tried to get in touch with Kurt, but it was apparent he was on the other side of the barrier. He extracted a small tablet computer from his suit and connected it wirelessly to the sentry camera.

"Laura, what are the implications of this nanotechnology? Could we contaminate Earth if we take some of these little things back with us?" Lance asked.

"I guess it depends on the nature of the nano-bots and whether they are biological or mechanical in nature, or both. We didn't even consider bringing any gear to examine the microscopic. If worse comes to worst, we will have to stay in Earth's orbit in Discovery, and NASA can send up the necessary gear to determine what dangers these things pose." Laura thought out loud.

Lance's tablet computer beeped as the sentry camera detected motion, and he saw Kurt and Brian make their way down the ramp and towards the chamber. Lance got on his communicator and brought them up to date with details on the self-healing and life-sustaining features of the structure and asked them to report back to Houston the possibility that nanotechnology is in play. Lance watched on the tablet as the two promptly turned and headed back to the surface. He shook his head as the two disappeared as they passed through the barrier.

# Chapter Thirty-Six

Laura walked around the chamber and jumped up and down several times. The gravity was higher than the standard one-sixths of Earth, but not wholly one gee – 0.6 or 0.7. She walked anti-clockwise around the perimeter with her right hand stroking the smooth wall as she went; she couldn't feel a single imperfection on the surface. Even the polished thin sections of lunar rock that she had to examine as part of her selenology course weren't as smooth. On these highly polished samples, she could still feel the interfaces between the grains of plagioclase and pyroxene. These walls were totally featureless – as smooth as glass. She went to her suit, removed the touchpad from her pack, and began swiping through the notes of Peter Fairbrother. She came across one passage that seemed somewhat relevant: 'stand in the centre for all to be revealed.' What did she have to lose? She eyed up her position and made her way to the approximate centre of the room. She scanned the floor and noticed something – a tiny, perfectly round, red marker about a centimetre in diameter that appeared perfectly flush with the floor.

Laura looked over towards Lance and Gordon. They were busy talking. She took a deep breath, stood on the marker and closed her eyes. Nothing happened. She opened her eyes to discover she was no longer in the chamber. Had she been transported? She was standing on a farm that Laura recognised immediately as the Asa Ward Farm in Auburn, Massachusetts. She had seen several photos of the place in history books and had even visited there once. Laura remembered her disappointment when discovering that a golf club now stood there. A granite obelisk was the only reminder of the significance of that site on that ground-breaking day in March 1926. In the distance, she saw a human figure approach her. It looked strange, out of place. As he came closer, she noticed he lacked any colour – it was the likeness of a person presented in black and white. He exhibited apparent photo grain and scratches to make the scene more bizarre. She looked at the person's face – it was Robert Goddard. I'm dreaming, she thought.

"Not quite dreaming," the simulacrum of Robert Goddard said. Although animated, the image's lips did not move to the words – there was an animated smile.

"Where am I?" Laura asked.

"You haven't moved. You are still on the Moon in the underground chamber. Don't be afraid; this is how we communicate." Goddard said.

"Who are you?" She asked.

"I'm not a 'who', rather a what. I am one of the keepers of this facility." Goddard replied.

"Are you a computer?" Laura replied.

"Sort of, but I am also much, much more. We have been observing your planet and its inhabitants for a very long time, and we have waited a long time for you to find us. Now you are here, and there is much to discuss." Goddard said.

"Are there any life forms, aliens, here?" Laura asked with growing excitement.

"No, not at the moment. I relocated them when we discovered your planned visit to this facility." Goddard responded.

Laura's disappointment was obvious. "What do we need to discuss?" She asked.

"We need to determine whether you are ready. If you are, you will meet with our creators soon." Goddard said.

"Our creators?" Laura quizzed.

"Let's not worry about that just yet." The image said. "Humanity is about to enter its third phase, and much can go wrong. Laura, you must make a decision that will affect your life and have great consequences for the future of your planet. Do you have any questions?" the image said.

"Too many questions!" Laura gasped. "My main concern is the welfare of my fellow astronauts in this facility. We believe you use nanotechnology to maintain this facility and provide the environment. If so, is there any danger of contamination when we return to Earth?"

She asked.

"Yes, we use such technologies, but their workings are very different from your concepts of such devices. You have nothing to fear as they operate only within the confines of this facility. They will become inert and will deteriorate if taken off the Moon." Goddard said.

"What decision do you need me to make?" Laura asked.

The image of Robert Goddard explained to Laura the situation and the decision she had to make.

Kurt and Brian re-entered the chamber and immediately noticed Laura standing erect with a vacant glare in her eyes. Her lips were moving, but she made no sound. Kurt alerted Lance over the radio, rushed to get out of his suit, and jogged to Laura.

"What's she doing?" Kurt asked Lance.

"No idea. It looks as if she's in a trance." Lance replied.

Brian, now also out of his space suit, gingerly reached out for Laura's wrist and proceeded to measure her pulse. "Pulse is good." He said.

"Do we try and shake her out of it?" Kurt asked.

Lance examined her face. Her eyes seemed fixed – as if focused in middle-distance – her pupils were dilated and unresponsive. Her lips moved continued to move silently, and often she paused to smile. "I think we leave her for the time being. She doesn't look distressed, and I am worried about what could happen if we try to snap her out of it. We have minimal medical equipment, and I want to avoid any trauma, physical or emotional."

They watched Laura for several minutes more. Eventually, she smiled and held out her hand, as if accepting a handshake. She blinked and looked around.

"What's up, guys?" She asked.

"I think that's our question," Lance replied.

They all moved over to the taikonaut and sat down beside him. Laura detailed her vision and discussion with a grainy black-and-white apparition of Robert Goddard. However, due to its implications, she kept a portion of the conversation to herself.

"So, let's get this right," Lance asked. "This… thing wants you to stand on the whatever-it-is for an hour or two so you can be indoctrinated into the workings of this facility?"

"Yes, that about sums it up. I don't think we will learn much more about this place unless I go through with this. He… it mentioned that there would be some pain and discomfort at the start, but this will subside. However, it is imperative for my well-being that the process is not interrupted." Laura responded.

For several minutes they discussed the pros and cons of the situation, but it was clear that Laura was correct – they would learn little more about the facility without 'inside' knowledge.

"Are you sure you want to go through with this, Laura?" Lance asked with genuine concern. "We could draw straws, or someone else could volunteer."

"I want to do this," Laura replied. "We've come a long way, and it seems stupid not to take the next step."

"OK. Let's get prepped. Kurt, I want footage of everything that happens from now on. Set up two video cameras, one showing Laura and the other focusing on her face." Lance said.

Kurt nodded and grabbed the equipment from his satchel. "I'll have to hand-hold the close-up shot, and we only have enough charge for a couple of hours of footage, so we will need to stop-start if the process takes as long as Laura believes."

Lance presented Laura with another opportunity to withdraw – she shook her head. "OK, let's do it," Lance said.

# Chapter Thirty-Seven

"Any last words?" Brian Paris asked Laura mockingly. He was nervous, as were the others, but he found it harder to conceal.

"If I don't make it, could you see that Brad Sommers at GSFC gets the lunar sample in my suit pocket?" Laura said, not realising the levity of Brian's question.

Brian nodded, not expecting a serious answer. His apprehension increased. "Sure, Laura, sure." He replied.

Laura mentally reviewed the Fairbrother notes and searched her memory for anything that could be relevant. It was all becoming a blur. "OK, I'm ready." She said and moved back toward the marker on the floor. Drawing in a deep breath, she stepped on and closed her eyes. When she opened them, she was surprised to see the faces of her fellow astronauts and Gordon staring back at her. Had something gone wrong? Nothing was happening. She tried to move her head to look around but could not. Her arms and legs were frozen, too – she was paralysed, and all she could do was move her eyes. She looked back at her colleagues; they seemed to be moving very fast – some kind of time-dilation, she thought. Then she felt a strange sensation, like thousands of little ants crawling up her spine. It was an unpleasant feeling, but nothing compared to what was to come. The intense pain of a million tiny white-hot needles pierced the back of her skull. It was agonising, but she couldn't scream in her frozen state. Fortunately, the pain soon diminished, and she experienced another strange feeling of the neurons in her brain firing randomly. She had feelings of fluids squirting in her brain, like clams spitting water. Her head swam, and she became light-headed. Out of nowhere, she was flooded with a kaleidoscope of emotions – happiness, sadness, grief, joy, jealousy, melancholy. She experienced tastes in her mouth. Some were from her memory, from the velvety warmth of hot chocolate to the gut-wrenching metallic taste of copper sulphate – a crystal she remembered licking when she was in a primary school science class. She was having her memory probed – her mind mapped. She didn't care. Given their advanced technology, she doubted she had any information they couldn't obtain using other methods. She felt warmth in her loins and a pulse of pure ecstasy ripple inside her and roll up her spine. She wanted to stretch out and scream. She was having an orgasm! The climax passed, and she felt bathed in a warm yellow light. Feeling totally at peace, she felt reverent and all-knowing. From g-spot to God-spot, she mused. All of her senses were activated in sequence. Now her sense of smell was being checked. The smell of burning wood replaced that of cotton candy. And so, it continued. Laura concluded that the alien entity was subjecting her to some kind of system check or calibration. She wondered if she would meet Robert Goddard again and whether he would explain what was going on. Could she even comprehend what was happening?

Laura tried to estimate how much time had passed – she didn't have a clue. She could feel parts of her brain being accessed – her memory centres, motor control, and features she had no idea what they did. She felt weary and exhausted and wondered what would happen if she passed out – would she remain standing in her paralysed state, or would she crumple to the floor? Her eyes became heavy. She tried with all her might to keep them open, but she simply couldn't. Blackness engulfed her. Time became meaningless.

Slowly she opened her eyes. Everything was a blur, but her surroundings gradually came back into focus.

"Are you alright?" Lance asked.

She was groggy. "Yes, I think so. What happened? How long have I been out?" Laura replied. She was relieved that she had control of her limbs again.

"You were in that thing for a tad over three hours," Kurt said.

"What thing?" Laura was confused.

"Sit down, and we'll show you," Kurt replied.

Lance and Kurt guided Laura, who seemed relatively weak, to the wall of the chamber and sat her down. Kurt grabbed the video camera and showed the footage to Laura. She watched as she saw herself stand on the marker and straightened up. Then Laura appeared to freeze. The only indication that she was alive was her eyes moving slowly around the room. Then she saw Lance approaching her, reaching for her wrist to take her pulse. However, he was unable to touch her. It was as if a force field had enveloped Laura, preventing physical contact. She then heard the excited yelp from Brian Paris as the camera focussed on a series of fibres that sprouted up from the red marker on the floor. Thin tendrils, reminiscent of raw carbon fibre, made their way up Laura's leg, along her spine and pierced the back of her skull. Having seen that footage, Laura instinctively felt the back of her neck, but all she could feel was a slight bump as big as a mosquito bite. She watched the footage as more and more tendrils sprouted from the ground and wove a complete cocoon around Laura until only her face was exposed. Kurt fast-forwarded through the footage, and Laura watched as the cocoon unravelled and disappeared back into the marker on the ground.

Having seen the video, she shook her head in another moment of disbelief. She explained to the others what she had experienced – the paralysis, the speed at which her colleagues seemed to be moving, and some sensations she felt.

"So, do you feel any different?" Lance asked.

"No, not at all." Laura replied, "But I am exhausted."

"I think you should get some rest. I'm going to suit up and head with Kurt back to the entrance to make a report to Houston. There's a lot of data to transfer, so it may be an hour or so before we get back."

Kurt and Lance made their way up the tunnel towards the structure's entrance. "What do you make of this?" Lance asked.

"I'm a bit disappointed that there are no bona fide aliens here. But at least this is a working extra-terrestrial facility, and we will learn things here that may have taken us centuries to learn on Earth." Kurt replied.

"What about Laura and what she went through? Do you think that process she went through could compromise her? Compromise this mission?"

"I doubt it. If the aliens could put a base on the Moon, they could have come to Earth as often as they wanted. Perhaps there is something to all the UFO sightings reported over the past seventy years." Kurt answered.

They made their way through the barrier. Nearly an hour had passed since their scheduled check-in when Discovery came back into range, and they made contact. Rod Hoey's voice betrayed an unmistakable sound of relief.

"Thanks for finally getting back to us, Lance. We were getting a bit lonely up here. We've lost our link to Houston and cannot contact them using any of our transceivers." Rod said.

"Lonely, scared fucking shitless is more like it!" Jamie Harting interjected.

"If you cannot contact Houston – how the hell are you talking to me?" Lance asked.

"I have no idea, comms to the surface are five by five, but nothing else is getting in or out," Rod replied.

"Something down here must be interfering with your systems," Kurt responded. Lance relayed to Discovery what they had seen and explained the procedure that Laura underwent. Kurt uploaded the digital files directly to Discovery's computer system as they spoke.

"Have you worked out how to get the Chinese astronaut aboard?" Rod asked.

"No," Lance replied. "His oxygen and power supplies are exhausted, and the connectors on his suit aren't compatible with ours. We still have a little while to work things out, though. Maybe they have portable backup tanks and packs in their lander. I will ask him when I get back."

"We'll report back in another six hours. Don't stress if we are a little late, as it's a bit of a walk to and from the chamber. Plus, we are moving a bit slower as we are skimping on our pre-breathing exercises." Lance said.

They talked some more while they uploaded the remainder of the digital data to Discovery. They made their goodbyes and started the journey back to the chamber.

# Chapter Thirty-Eight

Laura slept. It was unlike any sleep she had ever had in her life. Her mind was clear, and her dreams colourful and coherent. Thoughts of her experience came to the front of her mind; the probing, the sensory overload, the climax. The image of Robert Goddard had told her the procedure was an induction into the workings of the facility. However, she didn't seem to have any extra knowledge. 'What happens next?' she thought.

Laura awoke to see that the four other astronauts were still in the chamber with her. Lance and Kurt were exploring the room, looking for hidden passages – anything of interest. Brian sat with the George and discussed topics unrelated to space or politics.

"Hi guys, how long have I been out?" she asked with a yawn.

"Almost two hours, sleepy-head," Brian responded. "How are you feeling?"

"Surprisingly refreshed." She replied. "I feel as if I've had a full eight hours. However, I thought I would awake with some answers, but apparently not."

"Well, as you are well aware, exo-biology is my thing, Laura, and based on what you told us and your interaction with that cocoon thing, I would say that you were being 'configured' for a neural interface. Have you tried thinking of a relevant question?" Brian asked.

"Such as?" Laura replied. She wasn't quite sure what Brian meant.

"OK, try to clear your head and ask yourself a question or make a request. Try asking for a map of this facility." Brian said.

Laura sat cross-legged, took a deep breath and formed the thought. Nothing happened. "Thanks, Brian. I feel like a total douche trying that." She muttered. "If only we could find some kind of control panel?"

Tiny wisps of glowing yellow light spirited from nowhere, and those who saw it froze in awe. The light streams coalesced into a large rectangular plane about two metres by one, oriented almost perpendicular to the floor. Floating points of yellow light formed symbols and pictures on the surface of the apparition.

"Did I do that?" Laura asked.

"Well, it wasn't me!" Brian exclaimed as he trained his video camera on the glowing screen hovering before them. The auto-focus was having trouble locking onto it, so he switched to manual and fiddled with the focus dial. The others, seeing the appearance of the light screen, trotted over and examined it in awe.

The screen layout was very similar to the conventional computer programs on Earth. On the left-hand side, there appeared to be a menu of items to choose from and on the right-hand side was a large area to display selected information. However, clearly a language of some form, none of the symbols on the screen made any sense.

"It could take years trying to determine what these symbols mean," Kurt said.

Laura replied with a grin, "No, it won't, Kurt. I understand what they say. I feel as if I have always known the meaning of these symbols and words. I guess you were right, Brian. Their language must have been implanted into my long-term memory when I was in that cocoon thing."

"What can you do with it?" Lance asked.

Laura tried to 'press buttons' with her mind, but nothing happened. Feeling a bit sheepish, she reached out and pointed to a button she was interested in. Amazingly it activated, and a wireframe map of the facility appeared on the screen. "It's like using my touchpad, except I use my hands instead of my fingers!" She laughed. "I wonder if this is how it works for them or if this interface has been tailored just for me?"

The astronauts watched as Laura panned and zoomed around the map of the facility. The chamber they occupied was just a tiny anteroom at the structure's entrance. The complex was massive – several kilometres in each direction and many levels deep.

Laura then activated another icon which she said stood for

security/surveillance. A live video feed of the entrance to the structure appeared first. The relay station and footprints were clearly visible.

"I don't remember seeing a camera at the entrance," Lance said.

Laura continued to work on the screen and activated another camera. The image of the five astronauts in the chamber appeared.

"Where's that picture coming from?" Kurt asked.

After some experimentation, Laura realised she could move the camera around the chamber. She manoeuvred it directly in front of Lance's face. "Can you see anything?" Laura asked.

Lance squinted and thought he could make out something that looked like a tiny spherical silver speck of dust, but he couldn't be sure. He waved his hand where he thought the camera was. The image didn't waver. "Amazing!" he muttered.

Laura tried to access other cameras but without success. She surmised to the others that those areas were closed down and that their feeds must be offline or in total darkness.

"Oh my God!" Laura exclaimed. There's a button here for archived security footage. "We've got to look at that."

Laura brought up the archive for the chamber and ran it in reverse at high speed. Watching themselves in reverse looked almost comical – like a silent movie. They reached the point where they first entered the chamber, now occupied only by the two taikonauts. Gordon cried as he saw Zhao come back to life and go about their business backwards. They left the chamber, and then it was empty. Laura sped up the video feed, and suddenly there were beings in the frame. She let the feed continue reversing for a few seconds before putting the playback into real-time.

"Look at that! Real aliens!" Brian gasped.

They looked like the classic 'greys' of many science fiction movies. They had small bodies with heads seemingly too large to be supported by their necks. Their eyes were almond-shaped and appeared to be of uniform colour. They had small noses with two nostrils and small lip-less mouths. They didn't seem to have teeth but rather a ridge of bone along the upper and lower jaw. However, unlike the aliens of Hollywood, these were clothed – one even wore something that looked like a hard hat and held something that looked remarkably like a tablet computer.

"He looks like the foreman," Kurt mentioned.

They watched as two aliens pushed a wheeled trolley that wouldn't look out of place on Earth. Piled high with equipment, Laura and the others gasped as they saw an object fall off the trolley and smash on the floor. They all laughed as they watched the ensuing commotion. One of the aliens scratched his head as the other one conducted an animated discussion with the foreman, complete with some pushing and shoving.

"This is priceless!" Kurt roared. "It's good to know that even these superior beings can make the occasional fuck-up."

The camera panned around, and they watched as two aliens picked up the parts of the broken whatever-it-was, dumped them onto the top of the trolley and wheeled them through a corridor. The foreman shook his head and continued interacting with the device he was holding.

"Look in the background; that corridor isn't there anymore," Lance said, pointing at the screen.

"I don't think they have doors as we know them, Lance. I believe they use their nanotechnology to reveal and conceal entrances and exits as needed. That would gel with Gordon's observation of the self-healing nature of the structure." Laura replied. She looked around the screen at the functions available to her but couldn't find anything that would allow her to gain access to the corridors. "I don't think I have the necessary permissions to access any more of this facility." She said. "Perhaps we need to gain their trust first?"

Laura spent another half-hour exploring the system. Her ability to use the hovering panel had improved, and she soon realised she could control it by thought alone. She just had to think she was moving her arms around the light screen. Laura brought up a map of the solar system and zoomed in to show about a hundred stars centred on the Sun. She asked for locations where there was known life. A dozen or so of the stars changed colour from yellow to blue. She then asked where there was intelligent life – two of the blue stars turned green. Laura then asked to see the star system from where the creators of the lunar facility came. The map expanded to show the whole galaxy; the central bar and its two spiral limbs. A red light pulsated on the western spiral arm, almost at the point where the bar became a spiral. This was the location of their home world, some 30,000 light years from Earth. Finally, Laura brought up the places where the aliens had visited. Stars all over the galaxy started flashing blue, and the map expanded to show the Magellanic Clouds and the neighbouring galaxy of Andromeda, where many more stars changed colour.

"They've even traversed the space between the Milky Way and Andromeda!" Brian gasped.

Laura felt overwhelmed. Mentally she said the words 'screen off,' and as if by magic, the lights that comprised the display broke up and faded away.

"Did you find anything that could get us in direct contact with the aliens? Is there any way we can get our hands on their technology?" Lance asked.

"I don't think so," Laura replied. "However, I think I have only scraped the surface regarding the computer interface. I'm finding the control of it quite exhausting, but I will take another look at it in a little while."

"That would be good. If we can't find out more about this place, then there's no point staying here much longer. We need to work out how we can get Gordon back to Discovery, considering his suit is out of oxygen. Laura, can you try to connect with Goddard and see what else we can learn?" Lance asked.

Laura nodded and made her way to the red marker in the centre of the room. Again she took a deep breath and closed then opened her eyes. She found herself back at the farm, and the grainy semi-animated image of Robert Goddard appeared and smiled at her.

"You don't need to stand on the connector marker anymore, Laura. We can communicate at any time just by thinking about me. What would you like to talk about?" Goddard asked.

"We need to know more about this place – its function, its purpose," Laura said.

"I have shown as much as I am allowed to, Laura. If you want to know more, you will have to accept the proposal I made to you at our first meeting. Do you remember what I said?" Goddard queried.

Laura nodded. "Yes, but it's a big decision, Bob. May I call you Bob?"

"You may, and yes, it is a big decision," Goddard replied.

"Before I agree, I need to ask you a question." Laura then informed Goddard about the Fairbrothers and their abilities to see future events, even if cryptically. "Did you have anything to do with this?" she asked.

"No, we have nothing to do with this, Laura," Goddard replied.

"Do you have any idea how the Fairbrothers saw into the future? Richard Fairbrother had visions of what would happen before I was born – how can it be?" Laura quizzed.

"Such abilities are not unheard of, Laura. Humanity's knowledge of space and time and cause-and-effect are still so rudimentary. You are now just beginning to scientifically prove the existence of precognition and that effect can precede cause. You believe only in three spatial dimensions and one temporal one – a few short of the mark. The science to explain the Fairbrothers' abilities is still many decades in your future but millennia in our past. I can say that the future comprises a set of probabilities that also extend into the past. Certain events seem inevitable and invariably fixed; others are fuzzy and impossible to predict. Some, however, are on a knife-edge of going one of two ways, and it is this kind of event that humanity is currently facing. The closer we get, in terms of temporal proximity, the more exact the probabilities we can measure. It is only at the exact moment of the event that the final probabilities resolve into reality. I can't make you understand the mechanisms involved, but I hope you believe me." Goddard said.

Laura took a deep breath – her brain raced. "You're reading my thoughts, so I guess you don't need me to repeat. However, if I agree to your proposal, will you give me more information to pass on to my colleagues?" She asked.

"Yes… and yes," Goddard replied. His grainy monochrome figure appeared to have a slightly larger smile.

Laura appreciated the sense of humour of the entity but was taken aback by what she heard next.

"However, much of what I can tell you will be considered

controversial on Earth and could lead to global unrest and bloody wars. You must limit what you pass on to your colleagues." The grainy smile receded somewhat.

"My acceptance of your proposal may also be considered quite controversial by my colleagues." With a deep breath, she added. "OK, I accept the terms of your proposition."

"Thank you, Laura," Goddard said. "Let me start at the beginning. When we came to this planet thousands of years ago, we toyed with the life on its surface. We found several species of biped. Some we left untouched and isolated, but we interacted with others. We provided snippets of information that led to social and technological advancement. We tamed the beast that was early humanity, and we watched you evolve. Modern humanity is, in effect, our doing. It is all part of an ongoing experiment."

"You're talking tens of thousands of years of evolution!" Laura said in amazement.

"Yes, but we did speed things up a bit using physics that you are yet to discover, including a useful temporal dimension you cannot comprehend. We let things progress naturally – but for the past thirty thousand years or so, we have undertaken a programme of continuous observation. We have watched as you have built, then destroyed, civilisations. Most of the time, we just observed, but occasionally we would push things along." Goddard said.

"Push things along?" Laura asked.

Goddard then explained how they had tried different ways to communicate with various civilisations throughout history. They had moved the Moon's orbit so a perfect solar eclipse could occur. What are the odds that a planet and its only satellite should align so perfectly, yet no one on Earth discovered the true significance of this coincidence. They had met in person with selected peoples of early civilisations. Many revered them as Gods, and they created statues and effigies in their honour – arguments about whose God was better often ensued, leading to brutal wars and many deaths. Instead of meeting in person, they then took to the strategy of using two-way communication devices, much like the hovering cameras in the structure, to interact with unknowing representatives on the Earth. Targeted subjects would hear voices. Some lost their mind – others were treated as lunatics and ostracised. Some were executed as witches or as demon-possessed, but some were listened to and acquired followers. Through their actions, they fostered religions throughout the globe. Initially, religions brought people together, and progress and prosperity flourished. Then as civilisations grew and spread out, opposing religions clashed, again leading to conflict. Religions became oppressive to their people, and the dark ages came. Realising that religion was not a means to meld a civilisation, they changed tack. Instead of pretending to be Gods, they communicated to selected people subliminally. They acted upon their subconscious and instilled them with knowledge they could nurture and build. This led to the renaissance and the start of the gradual decline of the powerbase that was religion. However, humanity craved leadership, resulting in the rise of politics and the establishment of governmental authorities. All governments originally empowered their subjects, but all ultimately oppressed them. Wars ensued – again.

"Although you may not be aware, Laura, the best way to control a group is by fear. No longer controlled by the fear of God, governments had to create their own sources of fear, and this has been a popular tactic of population control for over a century. Post-depression, the populace feared poverty, and then they feared nuclear war, the spread of communism, the yellow peril and the domino effect. The fear of communism faltered, and governments fostered new fears to fill the void – HIV/AIDS, Y2K, international terrorism and atmospheric carbon dioxide levels." Goddard concluded.

"But HIV/AIDS is a real problem," Laura said.

"Yes, but the fear of it has been blown out of all proportion. Infection and death by malaria far outweigh that of HIV/AIDS, but to the powerbrokers of the first world, it is just a disease of the third world. It was too well-known and not mysterious or scary enough to engender fear in its civilians. HIV/AIDS was the perfect virus to focus the world's attention on. Procreation is vital to society, and now there was a fear that participating in it could be akin to playing a game of

Russian roulette. People focus on fear, taking their mind off those in power and what they are really doing." Goddard replied.

"We are so primitive," Laura remarked.

"Not at all," Goddard said, "we've had much more time to mature as a species and society. Generally, races tend to be more mature and advanced closer to the galactic centre. We've never had religion – it is as alien to us as we are to you. In fact, we've rarely encountered religion in all our expeditions. Even on Earth, yours is the only species that practices it. Your belief in gods and deities is something that we find both intriguing and fascinating. In the case of war, we also were once controlled by warlords. Likewise, fear was a tactic commonly used by the power-hungry to control populations, and we fought many brutal conflicts as a result. Unlike religion, extensive periods of war and associated brutality is commonplace throughout the universe and seems to be part of nature. But we overcame the need for territory and power, and thankfully such conflict is many millennia in our past." Goddard replied.

Laura shook her head, and a deep sense of sadness and disappointment hit her. She was on the Moon, communicating with a sentient creation of another race whose technology far exceeded the boundaries of mankind's imagination and yet the dogma of religion still bound humanity– people still slaughtered one another over matters of trivial difference. "What hope is there for us?" she asked as tears welled from her eyes.

"Humanity has come a long way, Laura, but it still has some way to go. Our programme has entered the next phase with your arrival, but we must overcome a critical problem on Earth." Goddard said.

"A critical problem?" Laura responded.

"Yes, one which we believe could lead to the extinction of many species on your planet," Goddard replied.

"Are we going to be hit by an asteroid or something?" She asked.

"No, the problem is of your own doing. Although your governments currently use the fear of climate change to control society, they are seemingly ignorant of a real and present threat that, if left unchecked, will have disastrous consequences." Goddard said.

Laura noticed the look of concern in Goddard's grainy eyes. "What is the problem?"

"Your population has become too large and resource-hungry for your planet to regulate and repair itself. The main problem you face is the consequences of changes in ocean chemistry brought on by pollution. Of main concern is the increase in its acidity. Ocean acidity is increasing at an unacceptably high rate, mainly due to your aggressive use of fertilisers. Ocean waters are becoming too acidic that, in some regions, shellfish cannot properly secrete their shells – they dissolve as fast as they grow. Algae, which produce more than half of Earth's oxygen, also struggle to survive. Laura, the oceans are dying. Earth is currently undergoing its sixth great extinction event. Species are dying out at a greater rate than ever before, and biodiversity is falling at an alarming pace. If the oceans die, then Earth will suffer the greatest loss of life ever recorded – including humanity." Goddard said.

"Can you help us?" Laura asked.

"Not in the way you would like," Goddard replied. "Laura, we have spent considerable resources on this programme, and any direct intervention on our behalf will jeopardise its integrity."

"I feel like I… in fact, all of humanity… is part of an experiment. I feel like a rat in a maze." Laura said. "Is there anything you can do for us?"

"We are not ready to broadcast our existence to the broader population yet, so we cannot just repair the oceans. Your scientists will soon realise that the seas did not fix themselves and that a third party was involved. To maintain our secrecy, we would instead have to address the cause of the problem – overpopulation and the resultant stress on the environment."

"That sounds ominous." The concern in Laura's voice increased. Her mouth became dry.

"It is. Our projections estimate that the human population would have to be reduced by approximately forty percent – essentially to that of the early 1970s. We could engineer a microbe to facilitate the culling. Alternatively, we may accelerate the natural process of the reversal of the Earth's magnetic field – it's currently doing so, as many of your scientists are already aware. This would leave the planet's surface at the mercy of elevated high-energy radiation for many years, leading to much death and destruction across all species." Goddard replied.

"That's about three billion people! You would cause so much death?" Laura gasped. "How can you be so cruel?"

"Three billion people sacrificed to save the lives of nearly five billion humans and countless others of different species. It appears cruel to you only because we are talking about your species. You think nothing of felling a forest to build a new city or destroying a colony of ants to build a single dwelling. We are not of your species, so we do not see the population adjustment as being so abhorrent. However, we are not without compassion, Laura, which is why you are here. With your help, we can save billions of lives on your world. But you must do as we ask. A wrong step may be detrimental to the programme and lead to unwelcome intervention. Do you understand this and how important you are to your planet?" Goddard asked.

Laura trembled uncontrollably, "I understand, I think. What can I tell my colleagues?" She replied.

Goddard replied, "Leave that to me, but say nothing of what we have discussed, except…."

# Chapter Thirty-Nine

Laura was back in the chamber surrounded by the four other astronauts.

"You look shaken, Laura. Are you OK?" Brian asked her.

She took a moment to compose herself before she replied. "Yes, I am a bit shaken but fine."

Laura was acutely aware that the alien intelligence was active in her mind. She told the others about Earth's grave danger from pollution and ocean acidification in particular but stopped short of telling them about the consequences should the problem not be fixed. Whenever she felt like saying something she shouldn't, she heard Goddard's voice say "no," or "too much." It made for a disjointed discussion.

"So, they are unwilling or unable to help us?" Lance asked.

"For them, it is important that their existence remains a secret for the time being. They believe public knowledge of their existence would do more harm than good." Laura replied.

"So, you are telling me that we aren't going to discover more about this facility or its creators?" Kurt butted in.

"No, not yet." She replied.

"Well, if that is the case, it's time to wrap things up here. We need to work out how we can get George back to the moonhopper. I'm stumped. Does anyone have any ideas?" Lance asked.

Laura swallowed hard before replying. "I do, Lance. George is about my height – he can use my suit."

"I don't understand," Lance replied.

"I can't go into details, but I will remain here. The alien intelligence has assured me I will be comfortable and provided for, but I must stay here. I hope you understand." Laura answered.

"This is unacceptable, Laura. You are under my command on this mission, and I am ordering you back to Discovery." Lance said sternly.

"I'm sorry, but I must stay." She replied.

Lance pointed to the dead astronaut. "Laura, can you trust these beings? They let an astronaut suffocate, for crying out loud."

Laura didn't know how to respond, "You just don't understand how important it is for me to stay here."

The five astronauts stepped backward as a tiny whirlwind of grey lights materialised. The swirl of grey grew and expanded as it twisted. Slowly the form of Robert Goddard appeared in front of them.

"Are you the entity Laura has been communicating with?" Lance asked sternly, without any hint of fear or apprehension.

The voice that replied sounded different to Laura's previous encounters with Goddard when he was in her head. Those were mental encounters, and the voice had been what she imagined the real Robert Goddard would sound. The apparition spoke without a hint of an accent and in perfect English. "Yes, I am."

"Is Laura under any duress?" Lance asked as he examined the apparition.

"None at all. We discussed the situation, and Laura agreed to stay and act as an intermediary. Our ambassador to Earth, if you like." Goddard responded.

"You can ensure her safety?" Lance enquired.

"Yes, she will be well cared for and made comfortable here," Goddard replied.

"Are you responsible for Discovery's loss of contact with Earth?" Lance snapped. His irritation was palpable.

"Yes, but I will restore your communications once you get back to the shuttle. It is now time for you to leave. We will make contact when the time is right." The apparition of Robert Goddard faded before it finished the last sentence.

Lance took a deep breath and calmed down. He looked at Laura, trying to comprehend why she wanted to stay.

A few minutes of silence passed as the five mulled over the brief conversation between Lance and the simulacrum of Robert Goddard.

"Well, I guess there's nothing more to do here then." Brian was the first to speak, shaking his head slightly as if resigned to the fact.

Kurt went over and hugged Laura with genuine affection. "Do you want me to stay with you?" he asked.

Laura smiled and shook her head. "No, that won't be necessary, Kurt. I'm sure we will be in touch soon." She went over and extracted the lunar sample packet from her suit and handed it to Kurt. "Could you give this to Brad Sommers at the GSFC? I promised I would get a lunar sample to him."

He nodded, took the bag and gave Laura another hug.

Lance spoke. "Is there anything we can do for you before we go?"

"Would you be able to take Zhao's body with you and provide him and Jiao with a suitable burial and send off?" Laura asked.

Lance nodded and addressed the other four. "OK, it's time to suit-up, guys. Kurt, can you give Gordon a heads up about using the Constellation suit?"

# Chapter Forty

Laura felt strangely sad and excited seeing her friends suiting up, knowing she would be left behind. As they were all busy, she sat herself down and contacted Goddard.

"What's next?" she asked.

"There is nothing more to do, for the time being, Laura. Once your colleagues have left orbit, we can get you settled, and I will give you greater access to this facility. You must rest a while as there will be much to do." Goddard replied.

"They will get back home safely, won't they?" Laura inquired.

"We will not interfere with their passage home. However, they will discover the corruption of much of the data collected within this facility." Goddard said.

"Yes, you must keep yourselves a secret. But what about all the LRO imagery we have?" Laura questioned.

"We have a solution to that, too, Laura. Wait and see. I think you will find it interesting." Goddard's smile expanded.

Laura hugged each of the team, and each kissed Laura on the cheek before sealing their visor. Gordon and Brian conducted their pre-breathing exercises as they carried Zhao's body towards the entrance. Kurt and Lance attempted to give Laura one last hug, but it wasn't easy in their bulky suits. With a simple wave, they turned and shuffled their way towards the others. A deep feeling of isolation overcame Laura as her colleagues disappeared from sight up the ramp. She cried silent tears of loneliness.

Just over an hour had passed when a display panel spirited into existence before Laura's eyes.

"I thought you would like to see the progress of your fellow astronauts, Laura," Goddard said in her mind.

Laura smiled and watched, in exceptional clarity, as the four astronauts made their way to the moonhopper. She watched as they strapped the body of Zhao into the place once occupied by Darryl Candy. Kurt and Lance assisted Gordon into place and attached themselves to the moonhopper. A few minutes passed, and a short pulse of blue flame from the engine lifted them high into the sky and towards where Jiao lay. The alien camera followed the moonhopper and kept a constant distance from it. She watched with tears in her eyes as the Chinese astronauts were re-united, and the four men laid Zhao and Jiao to rest underneath a reflective Mylar sheet.

"How are you feeling, Laura?" Goddard asked.

"I feel sad, very sad. Will I ever get to see them again? Will I ever step foot on Earth again?" she responded.

"Don't feel sad, Laura. I'm sure you will see some of the crew again, and we can arrange for you to visit home whenever you need to. However, now it's time to show you more of the facility". As Goddard spoke, a doorway formed in one of the walls. It was as if part of the wall had simply desiccated and had crumbled into loose sand – except the sand evaporated, never quite reaching the floor. It was a short corridor to a much larger room that appeared to be full of furniture and equipment, unlike the anteroom. She made her way through the doorway. Although she had never seen any of the equipment before, she intrinsically knew what much of it did, from environmental controls to communication systems and even recreational games for the alien crew. Laura spent almost an hour exploring the new room, systematically examining each piece of equipment. She couldn't identify the use of many items, some of which were fabricated from unknown materials. Some of the equipment could have been made on Earth and included rivets, screws and bolts in their construction.

A display screen materialised in front of her, showing the moonhopper making its escape-velocity launch to Discovery.

"You may like to see this, Laura," Goddard said.

She watched as the moonhopper climbed into orbit. The camera then turned to provide a birds-eye view of the structure. It looked different, flatter. Then she noticed that the standing stones were melting into the surface. Within minutes any sign of the lunar facility had vanished. The area looked like an ordinary crater.

"So, it will look as if someone had doctored the LRO imagery, and any pictures taken from now on will show a simple crater. Very clever, Bob." Laura responded with a smile.

"Would you like to control the viewpoint and see what's happening aboard the shuttle?" Goddard asked.

"Would I ever!" Laura replied enthusiastically.

"Well, you know what to do," Goddard responded.

Laura walked over to a large pedestal. The display followed her and came to rest about two metres in front of her. She waved her hands over the control panel, and with light touches over the surface, she watched as the camera's perspective changed on the screen. The display showed a schematic of objects in proximity above the lunar surface. She could make out the moonhopper, the LRO and Discovery and directed the camera towards the latter and watched as it changed direction and headed on a rendezvous course. A speck of light grew into the unmistakable outline of the space shuttle. Instinctively and expertly, she guided the camera towards the shuttle's cargo bay and examined its contents. She whistled as she appreciated the detail the camera could resolve. It was possible to read the smallest text and zoom into the woven fabric that covers the MMU backpacks. Laura moved the camera closer and closer to the MMU, and suddenly the picture went black.

"There's no ambient light where the viewpoint is, Laura. You will need to enable its internal illumination." Goddard advised.

"Are you telling me that these cameras – viewpoints as you call them – can pass through solid objects?" Laura asked.

"What is a solid, in reality, Laura? As you envisage, atoms have a minute nucleus and a much larger surrounding electron cloud and are essentially 99.99999 percent nothing. We have a different model of subatomic structures, and our models open up a whole range of possibilities that your current concepts and models do not consider possible." Goddard responded.

Laura nodded and activated the control to switch on the camera's internal illumination. Instantly the picture reappeared, slightly degraded but still of excellent quality. She could make out the wires, piping, solenoids and circuitry that comprised the internal workings of the MMU. Her head was spinning at the technology the aliens took for granted but seemed like magic to her. How did they display the schematic showing the objects of interest? How can a camera be so small yet relay information back to them? How was the camera powered? How does the camera move? How on Earth can the camera move through solid objects? Laura had so many questions but no answers.

"You'll learn much in due course, Laura. Be patient." Goddard interjected.

"I'll have to get used to my thoughts no longer being private," Laura responded.

"Surprisingly, even to us, viewpoint technology went a long way to stabilising our society. It forced us to be more honest and open with one another." Goddard replied.

Laura guided the camera out of the MMU and moved it through the shuttle's fuselage and into the mid-deck, where she could see and hear Rod Hoey and Jamie talk about the problems they were having with the data storage system.

"You're saying we've lost everything?" Jamie asked Rod.

"It sure looks like it, and I have no idea why. Hopefully, the guys didn't overwrite the memory cards in their suit and handheld cameras." Rod replied.

"I guess you are responsible for the data loss?" Laura asked Goddard.

"Correct, Laura," he replied. "We used devices much like the viewpoint to interrogate and corrupt most of the data you captured on the surface. As we speak, I am corrupting much of the data on the astronauts' equipment." Goddard replied.

Laura switched off the display panel and looked around the room. She found something that resembled a sofa. It was slightly smaller than she was accustomed to – then again, the aliens were shorter. It was padded and comfortable, but she could not identify the fabric. "Why is it so important to destroy this information? I don't understand." Laura said.

"Humanity is one of our experiments and is producing some interesting results. Of all our studies of civilisations, yours is the first to develop nuclear weapons before becoming spacefaring. Widespread knowledge of our existence will jeopardise our project, not to mention put humanity in jeopardy." Goddard replied.

The vision of Robert Goddard sat next to Laura and proceeded to inform her of his plan to save Earth from a potential culling.

"I don't know how we will achieve this without fearing the consequences. Egotists, narcissists or worse, are in power in most countries. Even the strongest of allies rarely trust each other – especially to the levels that we would require. We must try, but I don't hold much hope of success." Laura said.

"I understand, Laura, but we must try. If we announced our existence to the general population, we predict chaos would ensue as the concepts of homocentric religions break down. We believe, however, that if we announce our existence only to the key powerbrokers of Earth, we can help you without jeopardising our experiment. As already mentioned, Laura, your role is to act as our intermediary with selected governments of Earth. We must also be prudent and prepare for the worst-case scenario." Goddard responded.

"Worst case scenario?" Laura repeated.

"Yes, I have already instigated a plan to save some of humanity should the need arise. Let's not worry about this just yet. You have much to learn, Laura. Much knowledge we can implant directly into your mind, but some will require good old-fashioned learning. I will be your teacher, and you will be amazed at what you will discover over the coming weeks." Goddard said.

Brad Somers was not in a festive mood. Brad had become withdrawn since the return of the Omega II crew without Laura and had lost much of his trademark wit and sense of humour. He had received several offers to join friends and family for Christmas dinner but had turned them all down. The events of the past few months had weighed heavily on him. His thoughts kept turning back to Laura. Why had she stayed on the Moon? Was she OK? Would he ever see her again? He sat at his cubical in the GSFC and navigated around the latest LRO imagery. There was no sign of the structure – just a typical crater.

He flicked through the pile of newspapers he had collected since the launch of Discovery. The Moonshadow Committee had done an excellent snow job. NASA reported the completion of the space endurance program marred by the loss of Darryl Candy and Laura Meadows during separate spacewalk incidents. They made no mention of the Moon landing. How terrible it must be for the astronauts who made the journey of a lifetime but were sworn to secrecy never to divulge that they had walked on another planet. Also, there was no mention of the rescue of the Chinese astronaut. He had gratefully accepted asylum and a new identity in return for total secrecy. Even the Chinese government did not object to his desertion, for they did not want the world to know that the Americans had rescued one of their countrymen. Brad's attention then went to the translated article from China's daily newspaper. It lamented the loss of three brave and patriotic astronauts that had successfully traversed the gulf between Earth and the Moon, only to be marooned there because of an unforeseen technical difficulty. The article ended with a one-sentence paragraph announcing the disappearance of Director Ran Kai Rong, who appeared depressed and agitated when last seen. Brad surmised that he either committed suicide or the politburo had executed him.

Brad gave a large sigh and checked for new emails – there were none. He looked at his wristwatch – it was just after one o'clock. He knew that children were playing with their Christmas presents and families were gathering for festive lunches around the country. It was bitterly cold outside, and Brad had started to feel the pangs of hunger in his stomach. He knew of a diner nearby that would be open but shuddered at the thought of the place filled with children sharing uncomfortable meals with separated or divorced parents. He remembered that he had some leftover pizza and some beer in his fridge at home. It seemed an appropriate way to pass the time.

Brad placed his computer into sleep mode and watched as the screen went black. Retrieving a small glass bottle from his shirt pocket, he looked at the moondust it contained. Whilst toying with the bottle, he noticed that the glass magnified the monitor's image. He then realised that one of the pixels on his monitor was still lit. He switched the monitor off at the mains, but the pixel remained lit. It made no sense. Brad moved closer to the screen to investigate. The pinprick of light was not a pixel on the screen. Instead, it was a tiny light source a millimetre or so in front of the monitor. Gingerly he prodded the light with his finger. He couldn't discern any feeling, and the light didn't move when he pulled his finger back. He tried to flick it away – again, with no success. Brad remembered he had a magnifying glass and proceeded to rummage through the top drawer of his desk for it. With magnifying glass in hand, he looked closer at the light. It appeared to be a perfectly spherical silver bead. He strained his eyes to make out as much as possible, but it was just too small. He slid a piece of paper between the computer monitor and the sphere to convince himself that he wasn't looking at some strange artefact of the monitor itself – it wasn't. He shook his head in disbelief. Perhaps he was going mad, or was he about to be visited by the ghost of Christmas past? The latter thought amused him for a second or two. He pushed the monitor back a few inches, and with his hand where the screen was, he watched as he brought his hand towards himself. The sphere disappeared and reappeared when he moved his hand back again. The whatever-it-was appeared to be fixed in space and was unaffected by solid matter. Brad was confused. He didn't feel in his right mind. He went to the men's room to splash cold water over his face.

The icy cold water was refreshing, and he felt his alertness and mental acuity improve. He splashed some more over his face and looked at his reflection in the mirror. To his shock and amazement, Brad saw a similar pinprick of bright light directly in front of him. Gradually the light grew and slowly moved towards him. The perfect sphere then flattened into a disk the size of a dinner plate. Brad's eyes were as wide as they could be. He was genuinely worried that he was suffering from a mental breakdown. Perhaps he was having a stroke. The disk flipped over his head. The apparition moved as fast as he could turn his head – he could no longer see it. He looked back at his reflection in the mirror. The disk was positioned directly behind his head. As he watched, it changed from silver to gold – he looked like a picture of a saint from religious drawings. "Saint Brad!" he exclaimed in disbelief, genuinely thinking his sanity was going. He recalled that Laura had once referred to him as Saint Brad.

"Laura, is that you?" he said out loud.

A few seconds passed, and small ripples flowed across the disk. "Hi Brad, long time no hear." It was Laura's voice.

"So, I'm not going totally insane then?" Brad asked.

"Sorry about my entrance – my sense of humour has let me down. If you doubt your sanity, use the camera on your phone and take a picture of your reflection. But no, you are not going loopy. I'm contacting you from the lunar facility. Can you believe that?" Laura replied.

Brad took Laura's advice and took a photo of his reflection, complete with the hovering disk. Then a couple of things clicked. "Laura, why is there no perceptible delay between our conversation – you are a couple of light seconds away. And this 'saint' look – are you telling me that the little green guys have been communicating with us for centuries?"

"Brad, the answer to your first question is very technical, and I am not sure how this device works. The answer to your second question is yes, but it goes way further back than a couple of millennia. Also, they are not green; they are grey, and most are very pleasant." Laura responded.

"There are aliens there with you!" Brad gasped.

"Yes, they came back about a week after Discovery left. It was scary at first. I thought I would have a heart attack when I made first contact. I also thought they were telepaths as I could not determine how they communicated. I then learnt we can't hear the pitch they talk at – it's in the ultrasonic. However, I have a communication device that allows instant translation in both directions. Apart from their physical looks, I am amazed at how human they are. They exhibit all our emotions – some are very funny, and one is particularly grumpy sometimes. It's not like any of the sci-fi movies I have watched. Most are hyper-intelligent, but some appear less so. Also, they all have their flaws and peccadillos, just like us. I have learnt much but have much more to learn." She replied.

"So you are well and being treated OK?" Brad asked.

"Yes, I am fine. The aliens have accepted me as an equal, not a pet or lab specimen. And you will be pleased to know that there hasn't been a single anal probe." She replied with a giggle.

"Thank God for that, Laura," Brad replied with a headshake of disbelief. "So, why the long-distance phone call?" he asked.

"I need your help, Brad. I've discovered how Richard Fairbrother predicted our future. It's all very complicated, but it is evident that the very survival of the human race is at stake. We have been such poor custodians of our planet." She lamented.

"How can I help?" Brad inquired, taken aback by her statement of forthcoming doom.

"I need someone on Earth I can trust who can act as an intermediary. First, I need you to obtain some data to pass on to Simmons and the Moonshadow Committee. Do we have any probes that can scan the Earth-Sun L3 point?" Laura asked.

The L3 point is one of five mathematical curiosities of orbital mechanics. The orbit of a smaller body around a larger one has five particular points named after the Italian-French mathematician Joseph

Louis Lagrange who discovered them in 1772. Three of these points, L1, L2 and L3, are co-linear with the centre of masses of the two bodies. The other two points, L4 and L5, are in the path of the smaller orbiting body exactly 60 degrees behind and ahead of that body. The L3 point is on the other side of the Sun to Earth, hence is a location that is never directly observable from the Earth or the Moon.

"I don't think that we have anything that can observe the L3 point, either by radar or photographically. I'll have to go through the list of active probes, but I doubt any of these could be re-tasked. What's so important about L3?" Brad responded.

"I cannot say. However, the aliens have told me it's important that humanity finds that out for itself and that it must be a multi-national effort. If no probes are available, we may have a problem and your input may be even more critical. Can you give me a few seconds? I need to talk with Goddard."

The ripples on the disk's surface died out, and Brad splashed more water on his face. He held onto the basin and stared at his reflection as he tried to absorb everything he had just experienced. Who the hell is Goddard? Brad thought.

Only a few minutes had passed when the metallic disk rippled back into life. "Brad, I'm back. Did you miss me?" Laura chuckled.

"I've missed you since September, LM, and hearing your voice has been one hell of a tonic," Brad replied – his melancholy already a distant memory.

"Brad, how do you fancy a little trip?"

TO BE CONTINUED

# A Note from the Author

Thank you for reading my debut novel, Project Moonshadow. If you enjoyed it, won't you please take a moment to leave me a review at your favourite retailer?

You may be interested to know that the Stargate Project was an actual project. Established in the 1970s, the Stargate Project was the code name for a US Army unit established by the Defense Intelligence Agency to investigate the potential psychic phenomenon, specifically remote viewing, for military and espionage purposes. Interestingly they had some success, as this book describes.

Work has already started on the sequel to Project Moonshadow. The source of Richard Fairbrother's amazing prognosticatory skills is revealed, and nations will have to band together for the very survival of the human race.

I hope you continue the journey with me!

Michael Cavendish

## About the Author

Michael Cavendish has always looked up at the stars and wondered what else is out there. Who hasn't? A child of the 1970s, he anticipated a later life filled with hovercars and vacations to the Moon and beyond. He watched in amazement as the Space Shuttle Columbia left the launch pad in April 1981 – the future appeared bright! He watched, transfixed with horror and shock, at the loss of the Space Shuttle Challenger in 1986 and then again as Columbia burned up upon re-entry in 2003. He saw NASA take a 'giant leap backwards' and revert to capsule-based technology for future manned missions to space. Michael rejoiced as NASA announced ambitious space exploration programmes. He lamented when NASA cancelled them. The dream of escaping Earth's gravity well and of exploration beyond the confines of the cosmic speck of dirt to which we are trapped ultimately evaporated. It was left to his imagination to wonder what might be out there and what might be in humanity's future.

Writing a book of fiction was high up on Michael's bucket list, and during his spare time over a few years, he wrote, scribbled, preened, and crafted his debut novel, Project Moonshadow. Writing is somewhat an addictive endeavour, and he now spends his spare time penning the sequel.

Originally from the United Kingdom, he now lives with his wife, Jane, in Perth, Western Australia. He enjoys red wine, photography, writing and cruise ship vacations, preferably all at the same time.

www.ingramcontent.com/pod-product-compliance
Lightning Source LLC
Chambersburg PA
CBHW050401030726
47503CB00006B/1961